In the Coming and Going

In the Coming and Going

a novel in verse

Rachel Langley

This is a work of fiction. Names, characters, places, and incidents are products of the author's imagination or are used fictitiously and are not to be construed as real. Any resemblance to actual events, locales, organizations, or persons, living or dead, is entirely coincidental.

First Edition

Hardcover ISBN 979-8-9915796-0-5
Paperback ISBN 979-8-9915796-1-2
E-book ISBN 979-8-9915796-2-9

For the ones who mother and grandmother us

One

My conception was intended to fix a marriage,
the idea another baby would make them better,
happy or
whole.
I was to be a boy
since they already had a daughter.
Failure after failure,
they separated eight months after my birth.

Divorce often means two birthdays.
It's time for this year's celebration
with Mom.

"Don't do any disappearing acts,"
my mother warns, wagging
her finger in my direction.
"You *want* to be here."
She believes by saying it
she can make it true.

If she says it firmly,
with enough conviction,
she can impress it
upon my will.
I want to be here.
Here
is a restaurant I did not choose
on a night I did not pick
to celebrate my birthday.
This is the only night that works
for him,
the man she's seeing,
the one she wants to introduce
to us,
her daughters.

"Seriously, don't go anywhere," she says again,
she pleads, needing me to respond.

"Mom, it's not like she can help it if she does,"
my sister chimes in.
Our mother
closes her eyes, shakes her head, tired
of that excuse.
"I'll do my best," I assure her,
placing an arm around her shoulders,
giving her a squeeze.

Appeased, she says, "You really will like him."

"I want to."
I say it with a smile.
It is true.

We are led to a table in a private room.
"Only the best for my Angel," Mom says.
She's the only one who calls me Angel.
It's Lina, I always correct her
in my mind.
My full name, Angelina,
would be better
                than Angel.
Angel is something to live up to,
and I don't want the expectations.

Just as I say, "It's nice. Thanks, Mom,"
Gabby asks, "So, when's he getting here?"

"Any minute now." She glances at her phone
then, pulling up the selfie camera
to check her lipstick.
"He had a six o'clock class."
He's a biology professor.
My least favorite subject; I hope it's not all he'll
talk about.
My mother reaches over,
grabs my hand,
grips it tight.
"Stay tonight."

A third time,
the tone of her voice
and intensity of her eyes
bring tears to mine.
She seems
traumatized
by my leaving.

"Mom, stop," Gabby says,
glancing around, grateful
we are in a private room.
"You know she can't change her
condition."

Condition.
This is the word our mother
has trained us to use
when we are in public.
It leads strangers
to believe I am
pregnant. They congratulate me. But
there has never been
life in my womb.
"If it weren't for this condition,
Timothy would be here
celebrating with us,"
my mother says.
Pulling away her hand,
fumbling with her napkin,

unrolling her silverware,
every clink pricks
my heart.

Timothy is engaged
to someone new, someone not
like me. He will never celebrate
my birthday again.

It's better this way.

I blink back the tears
and suck in deeply.

They will not run, and
neither will my nose,
nor my feet.
Running
a finger beneath each eye,
I wipe away my endangered mascara
as the professor appears in the doorway.
He's tall, a distinguished kind of handsome,
perfect smile, full head of graying hair. There's
something familiar about him.

He insists we stay seated,
approaching my mother,
bending low and kissing her
cheek.

Her mouth stretches
ear to ear.
My sister shakes his hand, and then
he turns to me with
a smile and
"Happy birthday, Angel."
That name, from his lips—
did I convulse inside or outside?
Either way, my sister sees.

"It's Lina," she corrects him.
Then adds, to soften it,
"Only Mom calls her Angel."

Our mother shoots
daggers at Gabby,

but taking his seat,
he just smiles, saying
"I've only heard your mom
talk about you, so I didn't know.
Let me start again.
Happy birthday, Lina."

"Thank you," I reply.
"You can call me Angelina,
if it's easier."
Gabby kicks my foot
beneath the table,

a silent chastisement
for always trying to
make things
easier.

"Sorry I'm late," he apologizes.
"Class ran over. So many questions
before midterms."

"Professor Charles Scott,
at your service,"
my mother says
with admiration.

Professor
Charles
Scott.
Could he be
Is he the same one
who'd had an affair
with Bea?
She'd shown me his picture
on her phone:
them together,
in love,
a student and a teacher.
A special kind of
secret;
thrilling,

jealous,
scared,
lonely,
brief,
broken.

It had taken months
to glue her pieces back
together,
to delete the pictures
of them
together.

She hadn't known
he was married.
He didn't keep
any pictures in his office, didn't wear
a ring, had
his own place near campus. When
Bea found out, he said he would
leave his wife for her.
A year later, his wife divorced him instead.

And now here he is.
I don't 'want to be here.'
Don't do any disappearing acts.
Seriously, don't go anywhere.
Stay tonight.

My mother's words pull at me,
but I feel myself slipping and
as the waiter arrives,
I stand.
"If you'll excuse me,"
I begin.

"Where are you going?"
I can hear the fear
in her voice.
"Just to the restroom."
I smile,
touch her shoulder.
"I'll be back."

Her eyes are full of concern.
But not
for me.
Don't embarrass me, they say.
I couldn't count
the number of times
I have embarrassed her.

"I'll be back," I say once more,
as I shuffle behind our chairs
and stride toward the door.

A mother and young daughter
are exiting the bathroom,

holding hands and laughing.
It is genuine,
and pure,
something other
than what I know.

The woman holds the door
for me,
our eyes connecting briefly,
and I hope mine
convey the words
You're a great mother.

I blink, surrounded
by fluorescence and tile and
mirrors.
Your mother is great, too.
I smell the air freshener.
Maybe good. At least,
doing her best
with what she's been given.

I will try to do my best.
I will not leave,
despite my
tingling skin, and
the warmth invading
my body.

You're not going anywhere.
You will stay here,
in this restaurant,
the one you would not have chosen
on the night you did not pick.
I have work to do, deadlines to meet, not

my mother's boyfriend,
not my best friend's ex.

Deep breaths at my reflection.
My eyes, hazel like my mother's,
green and gold
all swirled together.
Timothy called them mesmerizing.

My
long sable hair is slicked back,
the high pony
going for sophistication,
not a strand out of place.
For the person who
is always out of place.
Timothy liked my hair free,
when the curls fell
down my back, so
he could trace them
gently.

As soon as I close my eyes,
I see his face,
and am no longer here.

The restaurant, the restroom
are gone. This is
my *condition.*
My best is never
enough.

Crashing waves, ocean breeze,
salt in the air. I am there.
The same beach in Mexico
where he'd proposed.
His knees, both of them,
not just one, in
the sand,
his beautiful mouth
professing
a special kind of
love;
sacrificial,
honest,
respectful,
open,
known,
consuming.

His face, lit by moonlight,
as mine is now—
the lights over the mirror
are gone. Like me,
with my *condition.*
Disappearing,
Reappearing.
A lifelong curse
and blessing of
being taken
from one place
to another,
what we—me, Gabby,
Bea—sometimes
refer to as *teleportation*.
But for my mother, it will always be
a *condition.*

I have seen so much
of the world in
all my years.

I'd enjoy it more
if I could control it.
I drop onto the sand,
run my hand over the grains,
then dig deep with my fingers,
remembering the words
that poured from his lips,

like a cup overflowing, showing
the way he loved me
then.

There is a couple far down
the strand, their laughter
now and again
reminds me of when
I felt that kind of joy.

I want to be alone.
Sometimes
I know what I want.
Timothy sang to me
as the waves inched nearer.
Stars shining bright above you
Night breezes seem to whisper
                    I love you…

The water black, claws
its way back from the abyssal
deep,
as I have done,
          after he said
          he was done.

But on this beach he'd waited
for my reply,

my tongue ready for
Yes, and
a kiss, but
I'd disappeared,
leaving him
in moonlight, both knees
in sand.
I appeared on a cliff,
in Ireland
or England
somewhere
I don't know.

The sun, barely breaking
over the edge of the sea,
I screamed into the wind.
From shore to shore,
I was sure,
my answer was
Yes.

I returned to him more quickly than
I have ever returned from another place.
But the look on his face,
his fingers laced
together,
were unwilling to hold mine, to be
together.

He and Bea,
my parents,
Gabby,
are the only ones who know
where I go
when I vanish.
The only ones I tell
about the city lights
of Tokyo,
the warm nights
in Bali,
the bright balloons
floating over Turkey.

I had, I have
never been sure who
will accept
my condition.
But I had been sure
about saying yes
to being his wife,
to sharing my life
with him.

"Where'd you go this time?"
he'd asked, no patience
in his tone because
I'd left him alone
on his knees. He's

angry. No. Hurt.
My lips ready to pour out
a million apologies,
but instead, I say,
"Of course, I'll marry you,"
my smile glorious as the sunrise
over the sea.

He'd remained silent
as I'd plopped down beside him,
grabbing his arm,
going in for a kiss. He'd resisted
at first, but the more I pressed,
he acquiesced, then responded in full,
pulling me into him, gripping my waist,
firm fingers cradling my head,
his mouth beautiful again,
lips joining with mine,
parting for only a moment
to smile, to issue the command
"Don't go anywhere."
I look to the ocean,
a wave coming in, but the tide
receding.

My mother has a theory
about my *condition*. She says
it happens when I don't want
to be somewhere;

my heart takes me away.
Her theory crept deep
into Timothy's mind,
built a home there,
painted and furnished every room.
It bought expensive rugs,
hung blackout curtains,
started a fire,
set the table,
set me up.

She had her theory to thank
for Timothy's absence
on this birthday
and the rest of them; couldn't let go
of the thought
I didn't want to be there
when he'd proposed.

"Something in you
doesn't want this," he'd insisted.
"Something doubts us."

I couldn't find it
though I searched and searched.
I couldn't keep fighting
to prove my love, though I wanted to
cling to him.

"I won't marry you," he'd said,
if you're unsure."

And how many times could I say it,
and be made to feel
like a liar?

"If you'd wanted to be there,
you wouldn't have left."
was the only truth he'd hear.

The couple down the beach
enter the water,
though there are signs
warning against
swimming at night.

The hotel where Timothy and I had
stayed, behind
me, is still lit up.
It is always a risk to end up
in places without ID.
I keep my passport in my purse,
left at the restaurant table
for my mother,
so she wouldn't think
I was going anywhere.
I hadn't *planned* to go.
It is never planned.

I wanted to do my best,
to stay, as she'd asked.

I stand and brush the sand from my trousers.
I don't have money for food;
my stomach grumbles with neglect.
The restaurant has food
and my money—
all the foreign currencies
I stash in my wallet.
It also has my mother, another
lecture, her disappointed face,
possibly tears.

I take a step and land back in the restroom.
My sister is sitting on the bench,
                    back against the wall.
She's on
her phone, not looking up at me,
unaffected by my arrival.
"You really did it this time," she says,
her smile illuminated by the screen.

"How long was I gone?"
The mirror shows
my hair, no longer sleek
but windblown, loose, wispy
strands curling around my face.

Gabby sets my purse on the counter
and extracts a brush.
"Long enough for dinner to be cut short.
Mom made the excuse you
were not feeling well, that we
should celebrate another time. She's
saying goodbye to Charles now."

Professor
Charles
Scott.
I will deal with that problem
another day.
Our mother bursts through the door,
already saying, "Is she back y—"
before she sees me.
Her eyes narrow,
two angry slits.
"Where'd you go this time?"
An echo.

"Mexico," I say calmly,
relinquishing the emotional floor.
"I'm sorry, Mom. I didn't mean to—"

"You're sorry." She shakes her head,
taking a seat on the bench.
I'd thrown a wrench

in her plans for the evening
—again.
“Do you know what it’s been like
to worry about you every single second
of every single day, since
you were little?
Never knowing where you are,
where you’ve been, who’s cared
for you?
I don’t know how you’ve made it this far!”

“Mom, she can’t help it.
You’re acting like she can help it.”
Gabby defends me.
She claims she does not worry, insisting
it is the joy of her existence
to be part of my adventurous life.
Her fear of flying keeps her
forever grounded.
“It’s not fun for me either,”
I say. “Ending up in strange places
with no money, no identification,
where I can’t speak the language.”
I am poorly versed in many tongues instead of
proficient with one.

“There’s nothing greater than a mother’s worry.”
Her eyes pin me to the sink.
My stomach rumbles.

I grab my bag and head to the door.
I leave before she can continue,
before I let cruel
and calculated things,
like daggers
and flaming arrows,
shoot from my lips.
Taming the tongue was the subject
of many Sunday sermons, but
I don't know how to tame it,
only how to run before
it sets things on fire.

At midnight, in my bed,
replaying her words,
sleep will not find me.

But the chime of my phone, of his
distinct message tone does.
A text.
My heart races and I am awake.
Each pitch-black letter shouting
from its box with
rounded corners:

Timothy

Happy birthday, Lina.

Two

"He must have unblocked my number."
I tuck in between
two pillows on the couch,
knees bent to my chest,
eyes darting from the phone
to Bea's face.

She only indulges me
—though not without sighs and eye rolls—
because it is my birthday.

"Why do you care?" she asks
with a determined stare.
"It's been two years
since you've heard from him.
Three since it ended.
And his profile says
he's engaged."

She could still see;
he blocked me when
he'd grown tired of me
apologizing, pleading, promising
any and everything in
desperate attempts to keep
a man who did not want me.
Pathetic.
Embarrassing.
It's better this way.
I am over it, over him.

But my chest replays the spark and thrill
of nervous excitement, his message
tone clearing
a pathway to the past.
My brain has built a bridge
between the sound
and my memories of him.
I have been conditioned.

First things first,
change his tone
to the generic one, thrown
into the pool of all my
casual acquaintances.
No. Block his number.
No, tell him not to contact me, then
block his number.

I get to block him
this time.
My fingers begin tapping the keys, and
Bea asks, "What are you doing?
Don't message him back."

She snatches the phone away.
"This is your day.
Let's enjoy it."

She's right. I sit up,
putting Timothy in the back of my
mind,
where he belongs.
"What's the surprise?" I ask.
"Where are you taking me?"

Bea considers it a
personal challenge
to take me places
I've never been.
She is always
disappointed
I can never take her
with me wherever
I go.
If there is a way to take
someone when I travel,
I haven't figured it out.

I have not figured out
a lot of things.

"We're taking a short road trip
to feel like we're back in Korea
for a minute," she says,
her smile and eyes both
bright with excitement.
"Should we only speak Korean then?"

We both work in translation.
She grew up on military bases,
spent time in Europe and Asia,
learning German, Korean,
some French, and Japanese.
Bea's mom is Korean. Bea
learns languages for fun.
I learn them because I need
to survive with this *condition*.

It's what brought us together,
as young teenagers in a language class.
Then we lived in Korea for a year
after college graduation.
She gets to do translation work in
person.
I did too, once, for a couple weeks.
But when I didn't show up for one job
because I unexpectedly

went to South Africa,
they let me go.
I work from home now
                    —more time alone—
translating movies, shows, books, documents.

We live in Atlanta, but Bea said
a short road trip, and
we head south, out of the city.
"Can you tell me where
we're going now?" I ask.

She gives me side-eye,
a teasing smile, a look that says
I can't believe you haven't figured it out.
"Think about what time of year it is
and what city we're heading toward."

I grab her shoulder and
squeeze. "Wait.
The International
Cherry Blossom Festival?"
I could cry.
I've always wanted to go.
But never made the time, was
never around, always
missed it.

This small town in the middle of Georgia
has ninety times more cherry trees than D.C.
I've seen the trees bloom there, in Japan, Seoul,
but not Macon, just two hours from my home.

We spend the morning walking down Third Street,
trees in full bloom, a lacy pink display
the whole way. We window shop and stop
at a new boba cafe
for tea and macarons,
then head to the park, where
we stroll for miles along
the tree-lined Ocmulgee Heritage Trail before we're forced
to rest.

The park is packed with festival-goers,
amusement rides packed with kids.
The Ferris wheel and swing carousel
rise above the rosy blooms.
All of it reminds me of Korea,
But not the time spent there with Bea,
an earlier memory.

"What are you thinking about?"
she asks, handing me
cotton candy, its colors
mimicking cherry blossoms
and sky.

"The first time I went to Korea.
Do you remember?"

"How could I forget? I thought
you were making it up.
It's the reason we met,
the reason you learned Korean."

My seventh birthday,
my first time in Korea,
Dad's weekend.
He came to pick us up,
but Mom wanted to switch—
to celebrate my birthday at home.
Dad had bought tickets to take us
I don't remember where, but he couldn't exchange
them.
So, he insisted.

Gabby had already grabbed her bag
and hopped into his truck.
She'd told me to come with her,
taking my hand, pulling.
But my mother ordered me
not to come downstairs.

Dad in the doorway,
on the porch,
coaxed,

“Come on, baby. Let’s go.”
His voice steady, calm,
                    commanding.
I wiped the floods
from my cheeks and nose,
feet plunging toward
my bedroom closet, door
thudding shut to shroud me
in dark as I tucked myself amongst the clothes,
finding warmth there,
my knees against my chest,
my face in the crook of my arm.
I could hear the muffled shouts, but not
for long.

The playful screams of children, faraway
laughter, and I open my eyes to sunshine.
A tall hedge of bushes,
some pink azaleas.
The distant clicking of wheels
down the rusting tracks
of a worn roller coaster,
its canary yellow double loops
towering above the trees.
If I had been more like Gabby,
they would have enticed me.
I would have jumped up and ran
to the rides,
created my own birthday fun.

But I burst into fresh tears,
not knowing where
                    I was, with no one
                                        to care for me.
A boy came around
the hedge; tan skin,
brown eyes, black hair,
older.
When our eyes met,
his widened with surprise,
if only briefly.
He went to his knees
in the grass beside me,
hand on my shoulder,
his face twelve inches from mine.

He spoke,
the only word I could catch was
my name,
mixed in among the others.
Angel, accented.
Who was he?

Only my mother called me that name.
His face and language
unknown to me,
he seemed happy, relieved, but
concerned, glancing
to see if others were nearby,

to see if anyone could hear him.
I had yet to utter a word.
He pointed at me and said, "Angel,"
then jabbed a finger into his own chest
and said, "Byeong-ho."
He did this three times
as I struggled to pronounce
his name. He smiled,
nodding encouragement
when I got it right.
He reached for my hand
to help me stand.
He kept talking, though meaning
was lost.

He moved to leave, and.
when I tried to follow,
he gestured me away,
to stay,
even pushing me back.
His touch was gentle,
but my temper still flared,
tired of everyone's instructions.

'Don't go with strangers,'
my mother taught.
But this one knew
my name,
knew me, had

showed me kindness,
then pushed me away.
          I let him go.
I'd be fine on my own.
I'd stepped around the bushes
to see where he'd gone.

A paved path
diverging
through the wooded park.
He was running one way.
I chose to walk the other,
toward the sounds of the fair,
brushing my hair away from my face,
my tears streaking
the sleeve of my shirt.

The people I saw
were all Asian,
and they stared.
Am I in China? I wondered.
I didn't know about geography
or culture,
but my dad loved Chinese takeout.

I was coming to a place
where the trees and grass ended.
The Ferris wheel, slow-turning,
painted like a fiery sun,

the double-decker carousel,
its lacquered horses royally adorned, rising
and falling to a lilting tune,
underscored by the squeals of children
on another ride, a striped rocket, like a Bomb Pop
pointed toward the sky.

I was smiling because
no thought in my child mind
considered I had no money for admission.
Only this
would be better than
whatever Dad had planned.

Strong hands grabbed both
my arms,
two men fitted with uniforms
and stern faces.
"Let me go!" I cried
while struggling against them,
trying to plant my feet,
as they lifted me
from the ground, taking me
back in the direction I had come.
People, at least a dozen,
watched,
clinging to their kids.

Don't go with strangers.
Don't go with strangers.
My mother's words.
But I wasn't going.
I was being taken.
New tears,
the taste of salt in my mouth
as I begged,
their fingers only digging in deeper
the more I fought.

I spotted Byeong-ho,
watching, itching to interfere,
but a man—perhaps his dad—
held him back.
"Byeong-ho!" I yelled, desperate.

I'd learned his name.
He would help me.
But the men dragged me away,
and as I looked back,
Byeong-ho was pulled away too.
His cheeks also wet with tears.
None watching
took a step toward us.
A kidnapping in daylight,
they took me
into

a different kind of custody battle
than the ones my parents fought.

I gripped the doorframe
as they pulled me
in, my final fight,
locking me in a tiny room.
I beat against the door,
"Let me out!" I demanded for
only a minute 'til
my lungs were exhausted,
and I was back in my closet,
pounding
on that door instead.
It opened,
and I fell into
the arms of my mother,
trying to catch my breath.

"Why are you in here?
You could have opened the door.
There's no lock."
She distanced herself
to see my face,
but I clung too tightly.
"Why are you crying? Do you need
your inhaler?"

"Stop asking her questions,"
my father's voice
from my bedroom doorway.
"She can barely breathe,
let alone speak."
He pulled me from her, and I let him,
picking me up, and I rested
my head on his shoulder,
face buried in
the collar of his shirt.
"It's okay," he whispered,
rubbing my back until I
fell asleep, my lungs
filling and emptying
in quiet waves.

For months
I lived in fear I would
end up there again.

But I never told them what happened.
They chalked it up to being
upset about their fight,
Unknowing or unwilling
to acknowledge something more.
unable to handle
the trauma they couldn't

protect me
from
—better not to tell,
          not to know.

Only Bea does—and not
all the details.
I never shared it
with Timothy. He would have
          worried even more
every time
          I disappeared.

I traveled to many other places after that,
but it would be five years before I learned
what language Byeong-ho had spoken.
I was twelve
and heard an old woman
at the Asian market.
The sounds of her words,
the rhythm and cadence,
brought back the memories
and froze me
in place,
I gripped the inhaler in my pocket.
She smiled at her grandchild,
and I witnessed the affection between them.
I wanted to speak like them.
And I grew to love Korean.

During our year in Korea,
I searched for Byeong-ho,
scouring the flood of faces
at intersections
on the internet.
What did he look like now?
Could I trust my memories
of his appearance?
The light brown color of his eyes
I remember best, like buckwheat
honey, flecked with gray.
I contacted a few;
none of them were him,
none of them knew me.
Perhaps he'd forgotten.

"Lina, we should head back,"
Bea interrupts.
"Gabby will meet us
at the apartment with takeout
and soju."

"Is soju a good idea?"

She wraps her arm through mine.
"Don't worry.
It won't be a Korea day without soju."

On the ride home, Timothy
sends another message.

How are you?

Three

"Let me get this straight,"
Gabby says, already
on her third glass of somaek. We sit
on the floor
around the coffee table,
eating and drinking.
"He messaged you at midnight,
and you didn't immediately reply?
You haven't said anything to him?"

I haven't told them about his second text.
I shake my head. "I didn't know what to say."

Liar.

My sister claps her hands slowly, three times.
"I'm so proud of you. This shows growth."

Cowardice.

"He doesn't deserve a response," Bea adds.

"I mean, doesn't he?" I pry.
They both freeze, staring at me,
appalled.

"You're joking," Gabby says,
pouring another shot.
"Drink until you forget you
asked such a dumb question."

"Why does he deserve anything
from you?" Bea asks.
"Because he said 'Happy birthday?'
Good for him, he can string
two words together after
two years."

Gabby rolls her eyes. "Exactly. And
you sent him more than enough
messages he never replied to."

My face flushes,
whether from alcohol
or mortification at the mention of
all my bids ignored.
My eyes gloss with
unshed tears as I stare down
at the dishes of food, as I try
to justify my actions again.
"I just didn't want to lose him."

"I know," Bea begins,
"but more than that,
I think you've been scared of starting over,
meeting someone new,
sharing your life—your *traveling*—
with someone new, worrying if
they would believe you,
or accept you,
the way he did.
He knew.
That's why you clung so hard to him."

A few tears escape,
rolling slowly down my cheeks,
like raindrops on a windshield,
chasing each other.

Gabby finishes her glass,
chugging down the last half of it.
She slams the empty cup on the table,
making the dishes clatter.
This topic and drinks fill her
with anger. "But in
the end, did he
really accept it,
accept her?
He used it as his reason
to break up, to leave."

"Let's not rehash,"
I say. "I don't plan to
talk to him, so there's nothing
to worry about."

"And you've had enough
of this," Bea says, trying to
take the soju bottle
from Gabby's hand.
My sister evades her grasp,
laughing in victory.
"It will be enough when I fall
asleep on this couch."
Fall is the right word.
I'll be picking her up
off the bathroom floor.
She's always
had her hands full with me.
When she drinks, it's
my turn.
She fills
our glasses again.
"You two, drink up."

Bea and I look at each other,
already feeling the effects,
not willing to make her more angry.

We take small sips to keep her
happy.
Happy
birthday
to me.

Gabby's on hands and knees,
trying to make it to the toilet
before she pees.
Unsteadily, I straddle her,
hands around her waist
to help her to her feet.
But she can't stop laughing
from the tickles.
She falls,
rolling onto her back, knocking
me down in the process,
beside each other,
our legs tangled up.

"Stop making her laugh," Bea says.
"She'll wet herself."

Gabby laughs harder,
"Too late."

"No," I stretch and curl,
crying laughing. "I failed."

"You had one job," Gabby says,
waving a finger in my face.

"So did your bladder."
We fall into a fit of giggles.

Bea says something
I cannot hear.
"Huh?" I ask between gulps
of air.

She repeats herself.
She sounds upset.
"What is this?"

"What is what?"
I lift my head to look, and
she is staring at her phone,
the glow striking her face.

And I know it can't be good,
whatever she sees.
I reach for serious,
pushing myself, slow motion,
onto my elbows, sitting up
though my body feels
heavy, my arms like jelly-
fish tentacles.

"What is it?
What happened?" Are
my words
clear?
I can't tell.

"This."

She turns the phone,
but she's too far away. I squint
to make out the image.
I glance at Gabby; her
eyes are closed, not interested
or conscious.
Grabbing onto the table,
I pull myself up and
shakily make my way,
falling, again, on the couch beside Bea,
taking hold of her hand and phone,
blinking
my mother's face into focus.
It sobers me.
She's posted herself
and Professor Charles Scott.
The moment I've been dreading,
so unwelcome, and so here.
"Lo siento, mianhae, jinjja mianhae,"
I apologize.

She snatches her things
away from me. "What do you mean,
you're sorry? What is this?
Are they *together*? You
knew about this, and you
didn't tell me?"

"I only found out last night."

"Is he the boyfriend she
introduced at dinner?"

I give a slow nod,
wanting to close my eyes,
to be somewhere else,
somewhere with warmth.
"I only found out last night."

"You said that already."
All I hear is
you betrayed me.
"You had all day
to tell me—No. You should have.
texted me the moment
he showed up.
And this caption: *Love finds you in
the most unexpected places.*
It makes me want to puke."

“Me too,” I agree.

She cuts her eyes at me.
“No. I think I’m actually
going to be sick.”
She rises from the couch and runs,
leaping over Gabby’s
body.

Sleep sounds good.
I close my eyes.
Let’s finish this
conversation
in the morning.
Morning.
So bright
and cold.
I wanted warmth, but
goosebumps creep
along my arms. No longer
soft velvet beneath me,
but hard earth.
I open my eyes and try
to sit up, slower than a sloth.
This is why I don’t drink anymore.
It makes me vulnerable.
Gabby and her good ideas.
Bea’s righteous rage.

I'm in the courtyard of someone's home.
Scooting back, I lean against
the concrete wall. Sleep
sounds good. I close my eyes.
Take me back, I plead.
My body shivers in the crisp air.
Not for the first time
I've arrived somewhere
poorly dressed for the weather.

Go home,
          go home,
                    go home,
knowing
it won't work. It never works.

I move several inches to my right
to soak in the sunlight's heat. My bare feet
the coldest part of me. I stare
at my toes through my eyelashes,
heavy, like my body and my heart.
They close, and I doze off
for a few seconds, few minutes,
few hours. Sleep devours
me. I can't count the time
or notice my stiff joints, numb skin,
can't get up to figure out
what place I'm in.

Screeching hinges startle me
                    awake,
the door to the courtyard opening.
Panic seizes me. Someone has arrived
and I'll have to explain my
trespassing on private property.
A tiny, old woman appears,
walking stick and bag over her
shoulder. I think, *if she's angry,*
          she'll be easy to run from.
Maybe. If my legs are in working order.
I try to assess how much I've sobered.
Toes are offline, but my bladder
is about to burst. Is there a toilet here? Would she
let me use
it? The house
is small and white with a blue door.
It is well-kept, but humble.

The woman sits down
on the other side of the yard, her back to me.
She lowers her bag to the ground
and pulls something out
—strawberries.
She eats a few quickly, as if in secret,
as if she hopes to consume them all before
getting caught. Every time
there is a sound outside,

she covers the berries and stops
to listen, only eating in silence.

I try to think
of the best way to alert her without
my presence scaring her, but
there is no good way
to let someone know you are in-
truding in their home.
This is my life. Scaring
an old woman, hoping
I don't cause a cardiac arrest.

I shift my weight, preparing to stand and make
my introduction, but before I say a word,
she hears me and turns my way.

Her eyes go wide. She gasps, but doesn't
scream. Her eyes narrow, squinting to see
me better, as she rises to come toward me.
I stumble to my feet, granting a bird's-eye view
of the snow-covered valley that is the top
of her head.
I take a few steps, closing the gap between us.

"Who are you?" she asks in Korean;
it's an accent I've never heard, but relief washes
through me at the familiar tongue. I'll be able
to explain myself.

If one can explain a magical appearance.
No, not magic.
Magic implies a magician, someone
in control.

Her gaze meets mine, and something like
recognition passes. Water fills her eyes
as she reaches up to cup my cheeks
in her hands, fingers
sticky with juice.
"Angel," she says
the name only my mother dubs, and I
wonder if she really knows it
or thinks I am the real
article, appearing in
front of her, like Gabriel to Mary. Should
I tell her not to be afraid? Instead
she cries, "Where have you been?
Where have you been?"

"Do you know me?" I ask,
overwhelmed by her emotion.

She must be confusing me
with someone else. Maybe
her eyesight is not as good
as her hearing. She drops
her hands from my face
and throws her arms around me,

crying harder. Between breaths,
she says, "I thought you were gone
forever, but you're here.
You're here. I'd know you anywhere."

Before I can console her,
I'm no longer there. Her head no longer on
my chest, my shirt soaked with her tears.
I'm standing in my living room, Gabby asleep
on the carpet, her hair across
a pillow Bea must have placed.
The coffee table is littered with empty bottles
and plates. The red numbers on the clock
tell me I've been gone
five hours. My feet track dirt across the floor
as I make my way
to the bathroom. Bea's bedroom door is shut;
I hope she gets good sleep, so we can have
a well-rested discussion later about
my mother and Professor Charles Scott.

But I can't erase the old woman's
face from my thoughts,
and her words—
I thought you were gone
forever.
I'd know you anywhere.
She must have been mistaken.

Dementia, perhaps
Alzheimer's.
I'm sure we've never met
but she seemed
to care deeply
for me. Or not
me, but someone who looks
like me, someone else she would
know anywhere.
What she must be
feeling at this moment.
I had been holding her
when I disappeared.
I wish I could have stayed.

Sitting on the edge of my bed, I examine my
reflection in the mirror above the dresser,
features barely visible in the streetlight
through the blinds. Even in the dark, I know I am
a mess. Sticky
from strawberry fingertips,
I should wash my face,
scrub my feet, take
a shower, brush my hair. Clean
myself up. Instead, I pull on a thick pair of socks
and crawl under
the blanket, home.

Four

Gabby sneaks into my room
shortly after sunrise, quietly opens
a couple of dresser drawers, in search
of clean clothes to wear, a pair
of sweats, and a t-shirt. I pretend
to be unconscious until she
takes them and leaves. The sound
of the shower running lulls me
back toward slumber, but it's not long
before she climbs into my bed
and cuddles up to me,
her hair conditioned
with a magnolia scent, falling
in gentle waves across the pillow.
I turn to face her. Her eyes
aren't like mine. They are deep
blue turquoise, like our father's,
and have always reminded me
of a tropical sea. I once
traveled to Greece, and staring at the

Mediterranean made me miss her.
She had been attending a doctorate program
in another state. I hadn't seen her
in months.
Her eyes are like water, something
necessary for living. That's what
she is
for me.

In the dim morning light, she whispers,
"I'm sorry I ruined your birthday."

"You didn't. It was fun."

Her eyes shift with doubt. "Really?"

"Mhm." I nod, closing my eyes again.

After a moment, she asks, "Why do you smell
like outside? What happened after I passed out?"

"I went somewhere."

"Where?"

"Korea, I guess.
The woman spoke Korean. Of course,
Korean people live in other places so,
I don't know."

"You didn't see any other signs?"

I shake my head.

"Hm. Well, at least it was somewhere
you could communicate."

"Communicating is good.
Being able to move and
think is even better."
I am, in fact,
annoyed at her for bringing and
insisting on the alcohol.

A guilty smile tugs at the corners of her mouth.
"I didn't think you had that much."

"Well, I wasn't peeing my pants,
if that's what you mean."
She buries her face in her hands.
"Just drunk enough
to end up in a stranger's home."
I've already had this conversation
with her many times before,
and it always seems like
she gets it, until she doesn't.

"I'm sorry. Really. No more pressuring
you to drink. I promise.

But it ended up okay, right?
You're okay? Nothing bad happened?"
She's concerned. I know she cares.
But she cannot understand,
gluing, as she does, collages
of my travels from
selected stills, a new
truth crafted
in the details
I choose to share.
"Right. I'm okay."

I feel myself
missing the old woman who
embraced me. Searching
for that same warmth,
I snuggle closer to my sister, though
she complains
because she's clean
and I'm not. The woman
did not care.

Of all my experiences,
this is new.
Where have you been?
Where have you been?
Had I truly
been there before?

I shake the thought away.
I would remember, if I had.

"I'm going to shower," I say, removing
the blanket and rising. Gabby pulls
it back, covering her
head. It's not long until she's asleep.

After showering, I pour boiling
water over a tea bag, and Timothy
makes my phone chirp again. The same
message tone I never changed yesterday, never
blocked.
It takes a minute
to find my phone, buried in the couch.
My dad sent me a message too, but I
skip it.

Can I see you today?

Timothy wants to meet.
I read the words through
shampoo-irritated eyes.
My silence is an answer;
he wants more. For all he knows,
I could have a different number,
could be dating.
But he persists and
I'm not sure I can

trust myself to see him
face-to-face. I hate
the person
I was
after he left me.
Would I become that person again?

Bea was right. He doesn't deserve
from me what
he so easily took away.

Let him know what
it feels like to be ignored.

All I have to say
is *thank you* and *I'm good.*

Ignore
every instinct
to give him
more.

No. I can't meet him. I have to
meet a work deadline. I twist
my hair into a bun, throw
on my shoes, pack
my laptop and headphones, and head
to a café
down the street. A change of scenery

always helps me
work more efficiently.
I can't think about Timothy
or the Korean halmeoni,
even if there is a woman in
the movie I'm subtitling who reminds
me of her. I think about her accent,
trying to place it, wanting to know
what region she might be from.
          As if I
will get on a plane and find
her.
The possibility thrills me
                    for a moment.
But I'm not
familiar enough with the dialects
to figure it out.

Two coffees and hours later,
I am almost done, when a hand lands
on my shoulder. I know
who it is without looking, my body tense.
I take a deep breath before turning
toward him, attractive
as he ever was. His glasses are new, framing
brown eyes I'm afraid to look into. It's been
about a week
since he's shaved; he knows I like it
that way. His t-shirt is tight across the chest;

he hasn't neglected
his workout routines. And he smiles,
a thing I used to believe was mine
but for two years, has been dispersed by wind.

"What are you doing here?" louder
than I intend. A few
people in the café glance in our direction.
He slides
the headphones away from one of my ears, like
he used
to do when he wanted to whisper
something flirtatious to me.
I pull
my shoulder away, pushing my chair from him,
taking the head-
phones off.

He's still just smiling at me.
"You didn't answer my texts, and I know
this is your Sunday workspace.
Thought I'd give it a shot."

"When you ignored my messages, I didn't
show up at your workplace."

"Actually…"
He takes the seat across from me.

"You did show up once.
You were really drunk.
You might not remember."

My eyes widen and my cheeks burn
as I do not.

"Don't worry about it."
His assurance does nothing.
He moves to apology.
"You're right. I shouldn't have come
without an invitation.
But I wanted to see you.
I miss you so much,
Lina."

"You're engaged. You shouldn't be missing
your previous fiancée."

He smiles, this one smug. "So, you have
been keeping up
with me."

I give him a hard look. "Congratulations, Timothy.
I hope
the two of you are very
happy."

"We're not together anymore."

He gives me that look, the one
when he's about
to tell me something very serious
and very true.
"I never stopped caring about you."

"When did it end?"

"A couple months ago."

His Facebook has not shared this news. I stare
at him.
When we got engaged, he was the first
to announce it on
his profile.
When he left me, it changed
to 'Single.'
All the questions he must have
received. Now, loathe to endure
yet another failure.

"What do you want from me?" I ask.

"I just miss you."

"I'm not who I was two years ago."

That's a lie.

I am exactly the same.
I have not made any progress. My heart

still wears half of a BFF
necklace; the other half I was
certain he'd discarded.

"Well, can we start again, as friends? I'd like
to get to know the new you. If you'll let me."
His voice is earnest, like his eyes.

I feel the tears building, threatening
                    to crash against
the walls I've built—a test of their
foundations.
I stand and gather
my things quickly,
fingers fumbling,
betraying me. He
grabs my hand
as if he is
allowed to come
                    this close to me.

I wrestle my hand free
and leave the cafe.
He does not follow.

At home, my bed
is empty. Gabby left. Bea's
bedroom door is shut tight.

I knock lightly before inching it
open.
Her bed is empty too
and perfectly made,
just like her military dad taught her.
I send a text.
She sees it,
                    begins responding,
                                                  then stops.

I should have told her about
Professor
Charles
Scott.

Of all the men in the city of Atlanta,
how/why did my mother end up
with him?
I stare at their picture,
the one she posted,
the one I could barely make out
through last night's blurry eyes.
The way she looks at him.
I remember Bea looking
the same way in a picture
she used as her wall-
paper.
Charming. That's what he is.
A charming liar.

There's a knock at the door.
It makes me jump,
the thought Timothy could be here.
But the fear and desire are for nothing when
I look through the peephole.

"Hi, Dad," I say when I open the door.
He has flowers and a gift bag, and open arms
for a hug I really need.

"Didn't you get my message?" he asks. Yes, but
I forgot to read it. Timothy's text had taken
precedence.
"I told you I was coming by," he says.
"Is it a bad time?"

"No, no. Come in, sit down. I'm glad to see you."
It's been months. I take the flowers,
thank him, set them
on the counter. "Would
you like something to drink?"

"I'm good, thanks." He sits on the couch.
"Looks like
y'all had plenty to drink last night."
He chuckles, assessing the mess.
I thought Gabby would have cleaned
before she left.

"Sorry about this," I apologize,
clearing the empty bottles and dishes, but
he stops me, his hand on my arm.

"That's not important.
It's your birthday. I can clean up.
You just sit down here and relax."

And I sit, as he says, thankful for
the moment of rest. "How have you been?"
he asks. "Have you been traveling much?"

A question any father would ask
his daughter.
He's direct, unlike Mom. He's never called
it a condition, hidden or ignored
by lack of mention.
Dis- and re-appearances not listed inconvenient.

Once, while staying with him
for the weekend, I vanished
for more than a day; Friday night and
all of Saturday, the longest I've ever been gone.
A country in Eastern Europe,
late evening. Though I had my bag,
my water bottle was empty, so I
went into a restaurant.
I sat at a small
corner table, people-watching and drinking

something, avoiding the men at the bar,
waiting to go home—
that's the last thing
I remember.

When I returned, I was injured,
bruises and cuts.
As a doctor, my dad treated
my wounds, but I refused to be
examined at the hospital.

I couldn't remember what my body
knew; each movement told me what happened.

DNA evidence is useless if
there's no proof
of travel.
No stamps in my passport, no
plane tickets in my name
to convict them.

And from that moment,
my father bore a new kind of fear.

It throws a wrench into my mother's
theory about my *condition*—that I only disappear
when I don't want to be somewhere. I certainly
didn't want to be there then.

I play with the fringe on a throw pillow,
twisting it around my finger. "I went to Mexico
Friday night, to the same place Timothy proposed.
And last night I think I went to Korea."

"Did you travel before or after you'd been
drinking?" There it is,
the look of concern, stern-
ness in the voice. He is always
the one who warns me to be cautious.
He understands the danger.

"After," I admit.
"Everything was fine.
I know
it looks like we drank a lot,
but I didn't
have too much," I lie.

He chooses to believe me,
for his own peace of mind.

"Is it happening more
frequently these days?"

I think about it.
"No. Maybe
just a few times
a month, like normal.

Perhaps more
this week because of stress."

"What are you stressed about?
Have you been practicing the
techniques we discussed?
What about a therapist? Have you
given that any more consideration?"
All the questions in quick succession
remind me of Mom.

This conversation is not the
rest I was hoping for.
He's switched to "fix" mode. Though
there is nothing he can do to
fix or control it;
nothing I can do either.

"Just a lot
of projects to finish for work.
And you
know I can't really talk
to a therapist; I could never
be honest or transparent
with them. It would be more stressful
to try and be careful with my words."

He's cleaning up the soju bottles.
"Well, you know you can always talk
to me about anything." He means it.
But it's not true.

He is dependable, but
I cannot depend on anyone.
When I travel, I am on my own.

I give him a nod. "I appreciate that."

Five

Bea's been gone for four days
and will not answer my calls.

My mother's dating
Professor
Charles
Scott.
I want to log into her account
and delete the picture of them,
take him out
of our lives.

I leave the café and
drop by Bea's brother's house.
She's probably camping out
there with her niece and nephews.
But before I ring the doorbell,
I disappear.

It's no longer
a warm afternoon
with clear blue skies.

I am here again.
The courtyard of the same little house.
This time, the middle of the night.
It takes time
for my eyes to adjust as they search
for light. When I peek
outside the open gate, glance
up and down the narrow, unpaved street.
I can see nothing beyond a wall,
stone and old wood cobbled together,
across from me.
There are no other houses, porches, or street-
lights in view
only the silent
dark holding the faint smell of snow,
a scent I did not learn in
Georgia.

I hesitate to explore. A stranger
might stand out
in a place like this.

Someone coughs inside.
The old lady with the strawberry
fingers had the same cough,

the halmeoni who'd clung to me
as if greeting long-lost family.

I sit on the step, trying not to shiver,
my ear cocked toward the blue door,
waiting for her cough to subside,
praying for her lungs to relax.
But it only grows stronger.
No movement or voice
of anyone coming
to comfort or help her.

She should not be alone.
Someone should come,
and I should hide.
There is a small building,
probably an outhouse,
around the back.
My stomach cringes at the
thought of hiding there.

The cough becomes violent and
I stand, unable to keep listening.
My hand grips the door.
I ought to knock, but not too loud.
Three soft raps I know she
cannot hear over the racket
of her body.

Cracking open the door—it's not locked—
I say in Korean, "Halmeoni, it's Angel. May I come in?"
Angel. The name I do not want
to be called.

Shining the light from my phone, I see her
in the corner, struggling to rise,
as she gestures for me to come inside.

I close the door quickly and quietly remove my
shoes, then hurry to her side, lowering
to my knees
on the hard floor.
Putting an arm around her
I help her sit up.
She's shivering, her coat and
blankets not enough.
A fever, a cold sweat.
She's hot, and the house is too cold.
In the opposite corner,
there's a small stove with a few orange
embers still burning. I wrap a blanket
around her small body.

She's crying again at the sight of me.
She tries
to speak between coughs, but I hush her gently.
"Let me get the fire going, and
I'll make you

some tea. Is there any medicine
you need to take?"

She shakes her head and leans against the wall,
her eyes watching me, her cough beginning
to calm, as if all she needed was to not be alone.
There's a small pile of wood stacked neatly, not
far from the stove.

"Use very little," she says, regarding the wood.
"It must be rationed."

I place two small pieces
into the mouth of the stove; it consumes
them as I stoke the embers,
but it won't be enough to get it going
again. I reach into
my bag, tear some paper from a notebook, set
the corner ablaze with the lighter I keep
for situations like these,
and place it beneath the wood.

One time I disappeared
into a dense and frozen
forest with no way to start a fire.
I thought I might freeze,
end up dead with icicles hanging from
my nose, no more warm breath to melt them.

I learned
then I need a lighter.
Halmeoni needs one, too.

She has a kettle with water
on top of the stove. Another thing I keep:
chamomile tea bags.
There is a tea set on the table.
"Is it okay to use this?" I ask,
grabbing one of the cups, holding it up,
the flames gleaming on the ceramic.
She nods. She's still trying to suppress
her cough. There's so much I'd like to ask her.

She asks me first, "Why are you showing up
here again?"

I almost spill the water as I pour it into the cup,
submerging the tea bag, watching steam rise.
I hurry to hold it beneath her nose,
warm, moist air
to soothe the congestion.
In the firelight, we stare at each other.
"I know," I say. "I'm sorry.
I don't usually go to the same place twice."

"You don't remember," she says.
"But you learned to speak Korean."

She smiles softly as she takes the cup
from my hands.

I give her two tablets from my purse.
"For the fever."

After she swallows them, I ask,
"What should I remember?"

"Kabi?" she asks. "You used to say
that word all the time."
I can tell she wants to
be sure.

Even with her thick accent,
I know who she means.
"Yes. That's my sister.
Gabby."

Her response
to my appearance was not mistaken
identity or delusion.
She knows me.

"When you were very young,
maybe two or three,
you came to see me more than
one hundred times. I always
marked it on the calendar.

You don't remember, but
you brightened
very difficult days."
Tears cloud her eyes again.

Young enough
to not recall.
I must have taken
more than I gave,
a small child requires so much.

She grabs my hand and continues,
"My husband and daughter-in-law died
just before you started showing up.
You gave me something
to worry about.
I thought I was imagining you, losing my mind.
A foreign child just
arriving every afternoon? I didn't understand
a word you said. I must have
been crazy."

An uncontrollable cough begins again,
her throat sounding so raw.

"It's okay, you don't need to talk," I say
words now she understands.
"Just rest. I'll sit with you as long
as I can."

An anxious look crosses her face,
but she lies back and closes
her eyes, holding back another cough.

I sit on the floor, lean against the wall
beside her. Her hand reaches
to hold mine again. It's tiny like she is,
aged and weathered, calloused, but soft.
I think of my mother's words.
'Do you know what it's been like
to worry about you every single second
of every single day, since
you were little?
Never knowing where you are,
where you've been, who's cared
for you?'

This halmeoni,
these hands—I memorize them—
took care of me when
I couldn't care for myself.
It's not long before she's asleep.
I tuck her arm beneath the blanket.

My bag is still on
my shoulder; I don't separate from it.
It goes where I go.
I take out the medicine and tea and
set them on the floor beside me, the least

I can leave
for her.

There's no service for my cell.
I snap a picture of Halmeoni as she sleeps.
I want to remember her,
in case I never come back
here again. Maybe I can
get on a plane and come find
her.

I don't have to rely on my condition
to bring me here. The sun will rise
soon. I'll go outside
and try to uncover this location.
Come back to her
                    one way or another.

I'm tempted
to add more wood to the stove,
but respect her request
to ration it.
I doze for a while, lulled with
watching the flames flicker.

When light seeps in
through the small windows, I wake, rise
and look outside. Snow has only

dusted the ground. I turn
to check on Halmeoni, but
disappear, returning to
the front stoop of Bea's brother's house.

But not before I'd caught a glimpse
of the framed pictures on the
wall behind Halmeoni;
the wall that held me as I slept,
sunlight reflecting off the glass.

Portraits of
Kim Il-sung,
Kim Jong-il,
Kim Jong-un.

Six

I sit on the concrete steps of
Bea's brother's house. Her car
is in the driveway now. It's dusk,
evening setting in, a hazy rose
gold sunset giving way
to the dark.
Though the sun still rises in the east,
illuminating pictures of
The Great Leader,
Dear Leader,
Eternal Leaders.
Their portraits on a wall
made of stone and wood.

I knew
Halmeoni's Korean sounded different.
I had been there more than
one hundred times. I only
remember these two.
The door opens.

It's Bea. She
sits down
beside me.
"How long have you been here?"
she asks, her tone masking
the anger I know she feels.

Three hours.
                "I just arrived,"
I tell her.

The year we lived in Busan,
we visited Bea's grandmother
many times. She told us stories
about her family fleeing
when the North invaded,
when Kim Il-Sung, the
Supreme Commander,
came south.

Although,
if the country had never been divided,
Bea would not exist. Her father
would never have been stationed
                            there, never met
                or married
her mother.

Everything I know about North Korea,
I learned from them.
But I am not here
to discuss there.

"I'm sorry I didn't tell you immediately,"
I apologize. "No excuses."

"Are you going to tell your mom?" she asks.
"Did you already tell her?"
Panic at the thought.

I shake my head. "No.
Do you want me to tell her?"
Panic at the thought.

She shrugs. "Maybe.
I don't know."

"Maybe the relationship won't last.
Maybe he'll see you in pictures with us,
get scared, and end things."
"Let's make sure to post lots."

"And tag my mom."

"Yes." She smiles mischievously, pulls
out her phone, scoots closer to me, selfie.

"Will you come home now?"

"My bag's already packed. Let's eat
dinner with the fam first, though."

Her brother Anthony, his wife Tamara,
and their three children, boy, girl, boy.
They're already seated
at the table when we go inside, and I am
welcomed as a part of their family.
The two youngest jump up
to hug me,
Auntie Lina!
Auntie Lina!

When Bea and I were in college,
we babysat them.
Bea left to see
the Professor,
and I played hide and seek
with the kids.
I crouched in their
parents' closet, behind
their mother's dresses.
But then I wasn't there,
appearing on a walking trail
beside a stream. Not a dream,
                              but a nightmare.
           I'd left the children

by themselves. Phone service-
less, I ran until a bar appeared.
I called Bea, who got
back to the house before I did. The kids
never knew I was gone. Except for the baby,
crying with hunger.

I knew then
I could never be
a mother.

An auntie can get away with more, can come
                                                                      and go,
and still be loved and welcomed home
with hugs.

No one has ever
discussed me
having kids. I wonder if they understood
          before I
did.

I cherish my moments as Auntie Lina.
And Bea has never been jealous,
knowing it's the closest I'll ever get.

Seven

At home, trying to work,
I cannot stop worrying
about Halmeoni. Staring at the screen,
tears blur my vision. I think
of her sick, cold, and alone.
What if next time, her condition
is worse?
Next time, I assume. But

there must be.

I need to be prepared.
I text my dad.
I met someone
in my travels, an old lady who's sick.
Maybe you know some
home remedies
I could use,
if I see her again.

What makes you think you'll see her again? he asks.
A second message quickly follows:
Have you been going to the same places?

A third message: *I'm nearby.*
I'll come over, if you're home.
I've triggered his concern.

Dad sits on the green velvet couch.
He was having dinner with a friend
when he received my text. I can tell
he's had a few drinks.

I sit on the floor, on the other side
of the coffee table, across from him.
"Dad, did I disappear a lot when I was two?"

It takes a moment before he speaks. "I was
in Virginia at that time, for residency. But
your mother would page me whenever
you went somewhere. Usually in the middle of
the night. Many nights."

Why didn't you take us with you?
I will not ask.
Residency in another state: an easy excuse
for marital separation.

"I couldn't help her. Or you," he confesses,
emotion filling his voice. I need to redirect.
"It's not something
anyone can help." I give
a light laugh.

He doesn't crack
a smile.

"Why are you asking about that?"

"The woman
I met, she said I visited her
many times when I was a child.
She took care of me.
Seems to…know me."
                    I pause.
"I've seen her twice
in the past week.
She needs someone
to take care of her now."

He begins to cry, hands covering his
face. It's out of
character. I realize
he is fragile, too. My strong, tall
father also tiny and traumatized.
My coming and going has hurt them all.

He rubs his face,
fingers running through dark
and graying hair. He pulls
himself together.

"Where is she from?" he asks.
"If she needs real medical help,
maybe I can contact
some doctors in her area."

"I'm not exactly sure.
I'll ask next time I visit--
if I visit again."

He nods. "Find out more information.
I'll help however I can.
It's the least I can do
for the woman who took care of you."

On his way out,
he says, "If you want to know more
about when you were two, you'll have to
talk to your mother."

Eight

Three days
worrying about Halmeoni,
wondering about a past I can't remember,
wondering whether I should
do what my father said:
talk to my mother.

Finally, I message her, make
plans to visit this weekend,
—as long as I'm here.

I've been researching North Korea,
waiting for the moment
I will disappear and see the blue door
of Halmeoni's house. Then I cry,
fearing I'll never see her again.

Ddok-ddok ddok-ddok.

There's a knock at the door.

I'm not expecting anyone, but
I know that knock. It reverberates
with familiar anxious energy.
The small, tight-fisted
rapping of my mother.

It's Thursday. I'm not supposed to see her
'til Sunday. I am working, messy,
crying over another scene.
The apartment is in no condition
to be seen. I'll use my condition
as an excuse; pretend to be gone.

Ddok-ddok ddok-ddok. The knock
comes again, harder, more insistent.
She calls out.

Ignore it.

She'll leave.

I breathe a sigh of relief.
But then the key is in the lock. The key
intended for emergencies.
I put the headphones on
as if my life depends
on it. I can pretend
I didn't hear her.

As she opens the door, she is talking
to someone. It's muffled to my

covered ears. She doesn't see me
on the couch as she runs to the bathroom.
Emergency situation, indeed.

If I hide, she'll just leave.
I won't have to hear her comment
about the dishes in the sink, the scattered
papers and clothes. I take
the headphones off,
gently close my laptop,
and begin to tiptoe toward
my room.
But there is a voice outside.

It's Bea. She's angry.
"What are you doing here?"

I rush to open the door.
Professor
Charles
Scott
has accompanied my mother.
Bea's body tells me she's somewhere
between fight or flight.
I grab her and pull her inside,
give Professor Charlie
an apologetic glance,
though I'm not sorry,
as I shut the door in his face.

Bea's eyes fill with tears.
This home we have
has been shattered.
My mother
is washing her hands.
We have two seconds, maybe three.
All I want to do is embrace my friend,
hunker down in a doorway and
wait. But
I drag her across the apartment,
shove her into her room,
and close the door in silence.

My mother throws open
the bathroom door, making me jump.
"Angel, what are you doing?
Didn't you hear me knocking? Why
are you not properly dressed? Have you
been sleeping all day? Are you sick? Is
that why this place is such a mess?"
In her dash to the toilet, she still took
note of everything.

I feel it too, the flight
or fight, the tears rising.
I push
my voice out in a rough whisper.
"Yes, I've been sick and lost my voice."

She steps away from me, toward the exit.
"Do you have a fever?" she asks, concerned
for herself.

"Not now, but I don't want you
to get sick."

"Well, Charles surprised me with a getaway
this weekend. So I came to visit,
since I won't be able to make Sunday.
Let's reschedule. Message me."

Her hand on the doorknob, she
suddenly stops. "Oh!" she says
as she turns back
to face me. "I talked to Sheila the other day."

Timothy's mom.
They had been close.
They used to talk a lot
before things ended.
"She said Timothy's been reaching
out to you. Have you seen him?"

I hesitate, but admit, "Just once."

I watch her hopes rise
like a helium balloon inflating.

I must pop it
before it floats too high.
"I don't think—"

"I do hope you'll give him
another chance. He's a good man
for you.
Just don't disappear on him again."

All my muscles tense.
She knows that's not how it works.

All the things I want to scream
line up in my throat, waiting
for their number
to be called.
She disappears through the door
before I can give her
a piece of my mind.

Mother,
then

My baby is gone again tonight,
her crib empty, the room quiet
except for this old rocking chair.
The wood is beginning to splinter,

too many winters
on my parents' porch.
I should sand it,
          right now,
                    at 2:17AM.

I dig in
the storage closet for sandpaper, to pass
the minutes as
I wait for my baby to reappear.
The only thing in which I place
my hope—that she will
keep coming back.
That, like the sun, she will return
every morning, ushering the dawn.

The mattress has grown cold
without her, warmth
that once lived inside of me, now gone.
Out there. Somewhere.
Where does she go?
I'd rather she travel back into my belly,
and have to birth her over and over
again. At least then I'd know
where she is.

Stephen wouldn't believe me
until he saw it happen, too.
The child vanishing

right before
our eyes.
"What will we do?" I whispered
to him. "What will we do if
                    she doesn't come back?"

"She'll come back."

"How do you know?"

"I just do."

His assurance did nothing.
His calm confidence made me
look
irrational, hysterical, unable
to accept my daughter's traveling.
What's wrong with her?
Is it something I did?
Gabby is fine.
                    What's wrong with Angel?

Nine

My mother
monitored me as a child, always
examining the expressions on my face,
whether I was smiling,
distant, or engaged in every moment.
When she asked, “Angel, is anything
wrong?” what she really meant was,
“Are you about to go somewhere?”

I heard her ask
so many times, whenever I
caught her staring, I no longer
waited.
“I’m okay,” I’d say. “Nothing is wrong
with me.”
It became the mantra of my child heart.
Even when I couldn't stay: I’m okay.
I’m okay.
I’m okay.

My mother is gone. I wait until
the Prof's
car pulls away before telling Bea
it's all clear.

She doesn't want to come out,
doesn't want to talk.

"Maybe now that he knows,
he'll end things with her.
And we'll never have to think
about this again."

"Let me know if that happens," she says
from beneath a pile of blankets.

I leave her, returning to work. But there is
another knock on the door.
Has
this man truly
returned for a conversation?
I will give him
a piece of my mind.

But no. It's not for Bea; it's for me.
Timothy.
We both must field our exes today.

Through the peephole I see
him standing there, a smile
and donuts I have not had,

since he left me.

I check my phone. He did not text.
Just like my mother said, nothing is prepared
for this. He's seen me like this before, but
that's not the point.

"Just a minute,"
I say through the door,
then rush to my room and
pick up some jeans from
the clean laundry on the floor.
The green sweater will do.
I run a brush through my hair
asking myself
why I care.

Because he knows me.
And I never could
stop caring.

I grab my bag, greet him,
suggest we walk to the park
nearby. He agrees, not asking why
he can't come in.
He's wearing the same cologne
I bought him years ago, the notes

of orange, sandalwood, and patchouli
fill my nose with nostalgia.
Think
of something to say.
"So?"
the faucet knob in my throat screeches
with rust. "Why did you
come by?"

"Because I miss you.
Just like I said before.
I've missed you every day
I haven't seen you."

"I feel bad for your ex-fiancée."

"She isn't you."

"That's very cliché."

"But it's true."

I grant him my eyes,
scrutinizing his words and
his intentions.
"Let's not talk about her. I came to discuss
us."
My heart beats
faster than I will allow it.

We sit down on an empty bench,
the streetlights aglow. A group
of teenage boys play basketball.
We watch them in silence. Or
I am watching them.
He watches me.

"I'm really sorry," he says,
"I ruined everything back then. I should have
accepted you as you are,
no questions asked."

Accepting me as I am sounds nice.
"You had the right to ask questions,
            but I needed you to believe
my answers, and trust me to know
my own feelings."

"You're right. I don't know
why I let the doubts grow to the point
I was willing to give you up.
Can you forgive me? Can we try again?"
When he sees my face, he adds,
"You don't need to answer now. Please
just let me know when you decide."

I change
the subject, ask about his mother, his brother,
his friends who were once mine too.

We talk about our projects and
eat the donuts he brought,
it all feeling familiar and strange.

It gets dark, and he walks me home.
We stop outside the door.

"Your bag has gotten bigger," he observes,
his fingers tracing the curve of it. "I've always
wanted to carry it
for you."

"But you can't."

His fingers trace the curve of my jaw,
tucking some hair behind my ear.
He's going to kiss me.
But then, I'm not there. I'm where
I've longed to be
for days. For a moment,
I want to go back. But then
            I stare at the three portraits,
the Dear Leaders. Nobody's home.
Halmeoni's not here.

When the front gate opens, I hurry, sure
that I'll see Halmeoni.
                                        I stop at the threshold.
                    He stops too.

A man in his thirties, standing
in the yard, his eyes hard as he examines me,
neither frightened nor surprised.
In such a controlled state, it is odd
he does not question my foreign presence
in the countryside. I should
be scared, but despite his cold stare, I sense
no danger.

He speaks first. "Halmeoni said you were back.
I had hoped she was just imagining things."
He closes the gate to a crack,
keeping his hand on it, keeping
his gaze on me.

"Do you know me?" I ask,
my word choice polite,
matching his formality.

"You *don't* know me?" he asks.

I shake my head. "Should I?"

"You should go home, Angel.
You're the last thing we need."

I can't go anywhere
even if I want to.
"Where's Halmeoni? Is she okay? She was sick."

His eyes become narrower.
"I'm taking care of her."

He opens the gate, and she comes through,
a smile spreading across her weary face
when she sees me. He
takes the bag from her shoulder. She
pats his hand. "Angel takes care of me too,
Byeong-ho."

Once she says his name, I can see it,
the little boy from my seventh birthday.
"Byeong-ho? I do know you!
I looked everywhere for you." There's
excitement in my voice, a mystery
solved, a boy found.
Just not in South Korea.

Byeong-ho helps Halmeoni into the house
and then leaves, the gate shut tight.
His last words to me: "Keep out of sight."

Byeong-ho,
now

The moment I first met her,
she appeared from nowhere.

I froze, my whole body trembling,
goosebumps racing along my arms
even though I was wearing a thick
sweater. *She's a ghost,* I told myself, closing
my eyes, willing her to
not be there
when I opened them.
She came toward me, and I pushed her away,
surprised that I could touch her,
that she was not
an apparition.
She fell down, crying.
Halmeoni burst
into the room,
          not shocked or concerned
          about me,
                    only worried
                              I had hurt her.

She had already visited Halmeoni
several times before
she showed up in front of me,
when I was home.

I doubted how human she was,
but she was not a ghost,
just a small child,
a baby, really. And I
hated her.

We thought she was older
because she was taller and chubbier
than most kids
we knew.
She just ate well
elsewhere.

Halmeoni had seen ones like her before,
met American soldiers during
the war. She said
                                        they were kind
            to her and the other children,
            giving them smiles and chocolate and gum.

She told me this every time she saw me
playing with my toy soldiers, plotting ways
to kill our enemies,
                          always succeeding in our mission.

Halmeoni didn't say these things in front
of my father. He knew she had a sympathy,
knew where it could get her,
get all of us.

She knew it too.

She only spoke about it with me.
And I kept it, locked in a box

marked *skeptical*. We were taught
to hate them.

The year I turned eight, she
appeared so often, I
expected her to be there
whenever I came home.
Sometimes she'd be sleeping soundly
and not wake up before she disappeared.
Other days, she would play with my toys
while Halmeoni cooked or cleaned.
She always left long before Dad
arrived in the evening.

Halmeoni would hang a scarf on the door
whenever Angel was visiting, so
I would know not to invite
anyone inside after school.

My friends, our food, and
Halmeoni were taken
by this child
who spoke only gibberish.

Her tongue makes sense now,
but my curiosity no longer
          scales mountains.

Our visitor's signal,
the warning scarf—
Halmeoni left it with me
                                                when she left me,
                                but
I lost it.

I walk back to the market
                                                to buy an-
                                                                other.

Ten

Halmeoni leads
me inside,
pats my arm and says, "Don't mind
him." The portraits of the Dear Leaders
pinned to her lapel catch the light.
"My grandson will learn
to adore you, as he did before."

"I don't think he will," I say,
but I remember the smile on his boy face
when he saw me in the park that day.
Perhaps it wasn't adoration, but
he had been happy
to see me,
then.

"Have you eaten?" Halmeoni asks.
When I describe to her the donuts
I've devoured, she raises
an eyebrow and then chuckles.

"You still have a good appetite, I see."
She pulls a few small items from her bag,

the best they can find
at the market, she explains.
I'm nervous, but
I pull the thing out of my bag
that's been weighing me down all week,
a gift of gratitude as a guest in their home.

"Angel, that is—"
Her eyes widen as she reaches
for it, and I smile softly,
setting the five-pound bag
of rice in her arms.
"A person can never have too much rice."
She cradles it like a baby and looks
at it as though meeting
an old friend
after many years apart.

Byeong-ho is gone just
long enough for
the rice to cook.
When he comes in,
he doesn't even look
at us, but heads toward
the only bedroom,
trying to ignore

we're already
sitting on the floor,
around the table,
ready to eat.
Halmeoni insists he join us.
He avoids eye contact, but
scans the table, surveying
the dishes before us.
But he says nothing,
his jaw tightening as
his fingers wrap around the bowl of rice
Halmeoni sets before him.

He eats quickly, whether from hunger
or a desire to leave.
Probably both, I think,
as I try to avoid staring. He has
a good face. It belongs to the boy I'd missed.
It's a good face, though his cheeks aren't
soft anymore.

When his bowl is empty,
he finally speaks. "What
made you come back here?"

"I don't know. It just happens."

"You don't choose where you appear?"

"No. I have never learned
how." I'm ashamed to admit this.
Halmeoni asks, "Do you go other
places, too? Where are you from?"

"I'm from Atlanta, a city in the states.
I have traveled many places, but
I've never been anywhere more
than once. Not like here."

"Why did you come to the park
that day?" Byeong-ho asks, his
eyes the same bright dark brown.
Halmeoni throws
a reproachful glance
he does not notice.

The questions are those
toddler-me couldn't answer.
But he isn't asking
to make friendly conversation.
It's an interview, interrogation.
"I'm not sure," I say. "It was my seventh birthday.
My parents were fighting, and I was hiding
in my closet. Then I was in the park
with you.

I don't know why."

"There are a lot of things
you don't know."

Halmeoni hits
his arm, a grandmother's warning.

Whatever he must think,
the lies he may believe,
he's right.

He continues, "Why did you say
you looked everywhere for me?"

"I didn't know you were from here.
When I was in South Korea, I looked
for you there."
Halmeoni is excited by the news I lived
in South Korea; she wants to go
over every detail. Byeong-ho takes
                    the opportunity to leave.

I stare at the door and
vow to make him adore
me again.
If I get the
chance.

Eleven

Gabby texts me Sunday morning,
says that Mom came home early from
the trip
with her boyfriend.

She says I should come over—
if I'm around. Says Mom's upset
because he ended things.
It's a good chance to show
her that I care. I can't disappear.

I crack open Bea's bedroom door,
tell her the good news. He went
running after running
into her.

"Give my condolences to your mom,"
she says. There is some sincerity
in her words; she knows

what it feels like to be hurt
by him.
I pull up to the house with a bouquet
and takeout from her
favorite Chinese restaurant. I'm grateful
to see Gabby's car out front.

Mom's sitting in bed, tucked beneath
a feather duvet. A barely audible episode
of *Real Housewives* plays on TV. I know
Gabby is the one who turned the volume
down so low.

Gabby gives me a look when I enter,
ones that says, "Please take over."
I don't want to,
but I will. For her.

"Angel, you came. Come, come
sit with us." My mom waves me
toward them, pats a spot at the
foot of the bed. Gabby is already
beside her.

I hold up the flowers and food,
a small offering to show
I come in peace. To give
any kind of comfort
I can.

After Mom takes a few bites
of lo mein, she bursts forth
with, "I just don't understand!"

She tells me how
he suddenly became
distant, not like himself,
he didn't even seem to be
listening to her when she spoke.
"And he always listened so well!"

She's been trying to pinpoint the
exact moment of change, what could
have triggered such an alteration
in a man who is, in her words, perfect.
I refrain from commenting

or vomiting.

In all her searching, she has arrived
at one conclusion. "It all started
after we went to your apartment.
You didn't say anything to him,
did you?" she asks.

"How could I have?"
She doesn't know I saw him,

unless he told her.

And, truthfully, I didn't say a word to him.

She fiddles with her nails and eyes me
with suspicion.

"Did you ask him his reasons?" I prompt.

Because the student
he had an affair with
is your daughter's friend?

"Oh, he just blamed it on work
and his aging mother. She's
the reason he left, or so he said. She
had a fall, and he has to take
care of her. He texted we
should take some time apart.
It's just what your father
said before our separation."

It's always 'your father.' She never
calls him by his name or refers
to him as 'Dad,' like we do.
Her tone makes the term
sound like a bad thing.
But she chose him
to be our father.

"Maybe he really does need to care
for his mother," Gabby suggests.
I'm guessing she's probably said

it several times
before I arrived.

Mom replies:
"Take some time apart really just
means let's never see each other again."

I hope.

She grabs the remote and turns
the volume up. "I know you girls are
tired of talking about this.
Let's watch."

Neither Gabby nor I insist
she's wrong.
I squeeze in-between them, and
we watch and eat in silence.
One episode later, Gabby is asleep,
leaning against the headboard. I slip a
pillow behind her head.

Talk to your mother, my father said.
But this isn't the time to ask questions.
This is when I'm supposed to
listen and empathize
and watch TV
while she cries.
But everything inside me

wants to fill in the blanks
of my toddler years.
Though
          her breakup pulls rank,
I can't keep quiet.

"Mom, can you tell me
about the year
I disappeared
a lot, when I was
two or three?"

"What are you talking about?"
she asks, panicking, like it's a secret.

"The year I would disappear,
mostly at night."

She stares at me.
"How do you know about that?
You can't possibly—
          Did your father say something?
                    What did he tell you?"

"He didn't tell me anything;
I asked him. He said I should
talk to you."

"What did you do? Some kind
of hypnotherapy
to recall early childhood
memories?
          How do you know?"

"Don't worry about how I know.
Just tell me—When
did I first disappear?"
It occurs
to me, this is the first
time I have requested
to discuss my disappearances
with her.
She hesitates.

"Just tell me,
please."

She makes a final flourish,
inhaling deeply,
before giving in.
"The first time I noticed
you were gone
was shortly after
your grandma passed.
Your father had gone
to Virginia for residency,
Mom moved in with us,

to help me care for you
girls. You became very
attached to her, and I
was jealous of the way
you loved her. Once she died,
you cried all the time
for her, inconsolable. I tried
to keep the same routine
she'd had for you, the same feeding
and sleeping schedule, singing
the same songs you loved, reading you
the same stories.
            Nothing worked.
I didn't know how
to comfort you. I slept
on the floor beside your
crib many nights.

"I woke up one night, and
you were gone. I frantically—
                    my whole body shaking—
searched the whole house,
the yard, ran down the street,
screaming your name.
Gabby was crying,
following me around
as I called the police to report you
missing, kidnapped. But when
they arrived, you were back

in your crib. I thought maybe
I was going crazy, from grief,
from exhaustion. The second
time it happened, I told myself,
you're just having an episode.
Wait for it to pass. She's there.
You just can't see her. So, I sat
in the rocking chair and stared at
the crib, waiting for the
minutes to pass. One hundred and
nine of them, and then I
watched as you reappeared.
From nowhere. From thin air.

"When it kept happening,
I took you to the doctor—a friend
of your father's—
trying to figure out what
was wrong with you, but
he tried to send me to a psychiatrist
instead. He contacted
your father,
told him I needed *help,*
tried to get him to commit
me. That's when I knew
how alone we were
with this *condition.*

"Your father showed up in a huff,
like it was an inconvenience to take
care of his family.
I made him stay up all night
to watch. We sat in
your room while you slept—
until you disappeared. Then
it was his turn to lose
his mind.

"He started keeping records, charting
the times you left and returned, how
long you were gone, if anything had
changed about you:
if you were missing a sock, if
your hair had been pinned up, if you
had food on your face.

"We tried to get you
to tell us something,
anything.
We argued about it a lot—
what you were saying.
But the only word we ever
understood was
'harmony.'
But how did you even know
that word or concept?
I wondered, is she disappearing

because we hadn't created
a home, a family that lives in harmony?
And I blame your father. It's his fault
for leaving."

I look into her eyes,
the same color as mine. "I wasn't saying
'harmony.' I was saying *halmeoni*."
"What is that?"

"It's Korean, for grandma."

"So, you were asking for grandma,
but in another language? Why couldn't
you just say 'Nana' like always?"

"I wasn't asking for Nana. I was
telling you about the woman
I was visiting
whenever I disappeared."

She gasps. "You
remember where you went?"

I shake my head. "No, but I have
been visiting Halmeoni again,
and she told me about
all the times I traveled to her."

There's a long pause.
First her expression is
shock,
but then her eyes narrow,
and something else,
creeps across her face.

"Why did you keep
going to her? What
did you need from her
that I
wasn't giving you?
Why are you going
to her
again?"

Oh. It's
jealousy.

"Maybe you should
just move to Korea
and live with her. Then
you won't have to travel."

I don't tell her how
impossible it is. I don't
tell her if it were possible,
          I would have already done it.

Twelve

The final frost has passed;
it's time to prepare for planting.
Halmeoni shows me how
she wants things done. "When
we first came to this town,"
she says, "I was clueless
about gardening, but an old farmer
taught me.
Not just how to produce
crops but a business,
how to yield
a profit."

This town is in a northern province,
two hours from the Chinese border.
My father asked again
where Halmeoni lives,
so he can contact nearby doctors.

Again, I avoided giving
an answer.
Byeong-ho already took her
to a hospital six months ago.
They did not have
the equipment or electricity
to run any tests. Traveling
so taxing on her body,
          she refuses to go
anywhere else,
though Byeong-ho repaired
their bicycle. Its old joints grind
through years of rust, but it gets
where it needs
to go.

Some days when I arrive,
Byeong-ho is not there,
having been assigned
to other tasks
because the factory where he works
doesn't work. It shut down
and no longer functions. I'm told
most days he sells goods
at the market, which seems to be
alive and flourishing,
just like Halmeoni's garden will.

Byeong-ho only allows me to work
in the yard behind the house
while wearing a netted sunhat
to better mask my features,
                    just in case.
The outhouse close,
a place to hide,
                    just in case.

I try
to make conversation, carefully
follow his instructions.
I smile at him
whenever our eyes meet,
which is rare. I am aware
how American it is
to smile so easily,
but it's earnest, my desire
to win him over.

Halmeoni aids the cause,
asking questions about my life,
encouraging him to comment
on what he hears. I speak softly,
                    in case
anyone outside passes by, but
sometimes my voice is louder
than I intend.

Byeong-ho is tense. My presence
worries him—and it should.
It is not safe
for them.
I ask them questions too, but
any answers they give
are clipped and incomplete, leaving
a well of things
unspoken.
Halmeoni's energy wilts
like thin leaves in
the afternoon sun.
Byeong-ho insists
she sit in the chair
he built.
She can supervise us, he says,
though I think
he wishes it were just him
she watches over.

Thirteen

Evening, near gloaming,
the sky is overcast, teasing
it might give
much-needed rain.
I sit beside Halmeoni
on the quilt I've etched into memory,
the blue florals faded from
years of exposure to the sun.
We watch a drama I've downloaded
on my tablet, though the foreign content
is illegal to consume.
When I mention it, she brushes
my concerns aside.
"Everyone does it," she says.
"Just don't get caught."
So we keep the volume low,
and the device securely in my grip, so
it is never left behind.

Byeong-ho is outside. He stays
in the garden whenever I come, keeping
watch, avoiding me.
Some days I join him anyway, fingers in
the dirt, clearing weeds.
Sometimes I bring him food and drink
when he won't join us for a meal.

Halmeoni has fallen asleep, her breathing
steady, but shallow. I stop the show
and watch her chest rise and fall,
wondering how much time
we will have. The worn hands
of the clock tick quickly here,
but crawl like a soldier stuck in mud
while I am home, reaching for my return.

The front gate opens. A man's voice
calls, and Byeong-ho responds. I rise
and move closer to hear what they say,
to determine if I need to hide,
          if the man wants to come in.

"I don't have anything for you,"
Byeong-ho says.

"Why not? This is the second time
you've been empty-handed."

"Halmeoni's sick. I haven't been able
to go anywhere."

"Get someone to take care of her.
I'll be back next week." It sounds like a threat.

I wait a few minutes to make sure
the man is gone before I open the door.
Byeong-ho sits in the wooden chair,
in the shadow of the house,
his head leaning against it, his eyes
closed.
"Go back inside," he says.

I step down and squat beside him,
looking up at his face.

"Go back inside," he says again.

"Who was that man?
What does he want?"

"Don't worry about it."

I persist, "Are you in trouble?
That man...He sounded demanding."

"*Life* is demanding, Angel.
That's all life is. One demand
after another
after another
after another."

It's the first time he's said
so many words at once.

"Can I do anything to help?"

"Stop coming here," he says.

As if his words are strong wind
I am pushed back
into the concrete wall, the coolness
seeping through my shirt. My whole life,
everyone has asked me to stay.
It's different—being asked to leave,
but I can't do either. "You know
I have no control over
where I end up."

He turns his head, looks down at me.
"Halmeoni calls it a gift,
but it's useless.
You can't bring Halmeoni
anywhere.

You can't bring a doctor
here. All
you can bring is yourself."

His words are an echo of
my own inner voices.
I want to cry, and the
            tears sting, but I beat
            them back.
"There must be *something* I can do."

He takes a deep breath,
stares at the ground, then back at me.
"Those shows you watch with Halmeoni—
bring me USB sticks filled with them."

"What will you do with them?"

"There's a market for everything.
            And don't tell Halmeoni."

Byeong-ho,
now

I stay in the yard when she's here
in case someone comes. I can stop
them, keep them from getting

too close. She's the biggest secret I've ever kept,
bigger than all the crimes I've committed,
all the laws I've broken.

Why do I have to,
                                        want to,
keep her safe
when all she does
is put
us in danger?

Fourteen

The Reactionary Ideology and Culture
Rejection Law, Article 7: "The State shall enforce
strict legal sanctions up to and
including the death penalty
against any citizen bringing in, viewing,
or distributing reactionary ideology and culture,
depending on the severity,
regardless of the reason
or the offender's social class."

Any person who brings in, possesses,
views, listens to,
or distributes
media from what is considered
hostile countries—
what he's asked me to do
could get him—both of them—sentenced
to reform through labor or killed.
It could also help them survive.

The serious language of the law in opposition
to Halmeoni's nonchalance, cautious,
                                        but not thwarted,
play a dangerous tug-of-war game in my mind.
Byeong-ho's request leading their side,
                                                    pulling the rope
                                                              to cross the line.

Fifteen

When I arrive,
Halmeoni is pacing in the yard.
Byeong-ho did not return
yesterday, like he said he would
the last time they spoke. His cell phone
must be dead.

I prepare dinner and watch her
through the window. Each step
she takes piles another stone
heavy in my chest.

“He’s never been late before,”
she says. I coax her through the door,
her eyes glassy with
unshed tears.

“Where is he?” she frets
as I wash her plate.

The squeaking of
the gate makes me drop the dish.
Halmeoni rushes to the door while
I wait for confirmation. She nods. "It's him."

The stones in my chest fall away one by one
at the sight of him. Our eyes meet
as he locks the gate. He seems relieved
to see me too. His clothes look clean,
but he's trying to mask a limp.
He smiles at Halmeoni, apologizes
for being late. She asks if he's eaten.

He eats like it has been days
since his last meal. Halmeoni waits
until he's done before unleashing
her questions and concerns. He avoids
most of them, only willing to say
he was delayed on the way
home, that he had to hide
for a while until it was clear.

She tells him he's not allowed
to go anywhere anymore.
She says I can bring them things
to sell at the market.

"As long as Lina comes,
you don't travel."

He gives me
a curious, knowing look,
reminding me of what he asked me to bring.
He rises and withdraws without another word.

Once the dishes are clean,
and Halmeoni's anxiety
has been allayed, leaving the Dear Leaders
to watch over her,
I go outside.

Byeong-ho is carrying
a bucket of water,
one side of his pants rolled up, the leg
scraped and bloody, his ankle blooming
with purples and blues.
He rolls his eyes at the sight of me
and sits down in the chair.
I want to get a good look
before the sun fades. I kneel
and take hold of his leg,
turning it toward the light.

"What are you doing?"
he complains, startled by my touch,
and tries to push me away.

"How did this happen?" I ask,
pulling the first aid kit
from my bag.

"Leave it," he says. "I've got it.
I'll do it myself."

"This is better," I tell him, not trusting
the water. He allows me to care for him,
lets me clean the wounds, covering
them and wrapping his ankle.

"How did this happen?" I ask again.

He hesitates.
"I had to jump
          from a train
I didn't have permission
to be on. I've done it before.
I just didn't land well this time."

"Byeong-ho," I begin,
but he stands and says, "Let's go in."
We sit beside each other
at the foot of Halmeoni's
mattress while she sleeps. There's
peace across her face, her
furrowed brow softened with contentment.

We listen to a
South Korean broadcast
on their NoteTel, a device from China
with USB and SD ports, able
to play DVDs, containing
radio and television tuners.
Each of us use one earbud.

He asks me to tell him
what's really happening
in the world.

Then asks again for the USBs,
adding SD cards to the order.

Sixteen

Gabby sprawls across the green velvet couch,
the first piece of furniture I purchased
for this apartment. It's worn-in, well-loved, while
I am worn out; well-loved, even
                    if I don't feel it.

She came over after work; Friday after school
lets out is her favorite time of the week. She
wants to go see a movie. I'm forced to
          admit I'm going
                    to dinner with Timothy.

She straightens.
"Excuse me?
When did this happen?"

"Only recently," I say it
with all the nonchalance
I can muster.

"You're back together?"
She's trying so hard
not to judge.

I shake my head. "He wants
to be. I'm still
deciding."

I jump in the shower
to escape more questions,
give myself time to think
of responses.
Timothy's been persistent, and I have
been open to his persistence.
That's all.

But her next question isn't about him.
"Have you really been going to
Korea a lot lately?"

Did Dad tell her?
"Why do you ask?"

"Mom mentioned it, in passing.
I meant to ask you about it sooner."

We stare at each other.
"Just a few times," I say.

"What are these pictures?"
She holds up my phone and
swipes through:
Halmeoni and me, Byeong-ho
working in the garden, ignoring
my pleas, their little house.
"They span more than a month."

I snatch it from her. "Why
did you go through my phone?"

"Your passcode
shouldn't be so easy. Your traveling
was never a secret before. Why now?
Who are they?"

"I don't have time for this.
Timothy will be here soon."

"Give me
the short version."

Running
my fingers through the tangles
of my hair, I say, "They're
the people who took care of me
when I was young, and I've been
visiting them again."

She scrutinizes me.
"That sign in the field. It looks
like a propaganda poster."

We study each other for a
long, quiet moment.

"What does it say?"
she asks.
She comes to stand beside me,
tries to scroll to the picture, but I pull
my phone out of her reach. "Please,
read it to me."

I don't need to look at it.
I already know
what it says.
전투적 과업을 철저히 관철하자!
Let us stay fully prepared
to fight!
I say 'fully' but the word holds more
than that:
a complete, exhaustive dedication.
A message aimed
at a people encouraged
to be ready for battle.

"I haven't been going
to South Korea."

Her cheeks blanch. "You can't
go to North Korea, Lina!
What if you get caught?" Tears
pool in her eyes.

"How long do you think I'll
stay in a prison?" I ask
lightheartedly. "I'm more
worried about Halmeoni and Byeong-ho,
who can't leave if
          I get them in trouble."

"Well, I'm more worried about
                              you.
                    Who else knows?"

"Just Bea.
          And keep it that way,
                                        okay?"

Seventeen

The house is empty when I arrive.
The rule we've made: I stay inside
if they're not home.
I cannot sit in the garden
to enjoy the morning sun. But
I'm grateful it is there,
to be enjoyed
by all of us, everywhere.
Sunlight has no borders.
No country can

claim it,

constrain it,

shoot it down.

Sitting on the floral quilt, I study
the portraits of Kim Il-sung,
Kim Jong-il, Kim Jong-un,
a reign
of seventy-six years
between them, an entire lifetime.

I wonder if it will end
during mine.

The gate screeches as it opens.
Byeong-ho hasn't fixed it
on purpose. The voices of two
women—neither of them
Halmeoni—carry across the yard.
They laugh. They stop
to observe the garden and remark
on its growth.
They approach the door, knock loudly,
call out for Halmeoni,
but receive no reply.
It's my cue to hide, as they let
themselves in.

I slip into Byeong-ho's room.
He doesn't like me in here, though
there isn't much to see.
I tuck myself away in the armoire.
From the inside, I can't
pull it closed. It hangs ajar, making my heart beat
faster. Halmeoni and Byeong-ho share this
wardrobe, but there's only
a handful of items to cover me,
knees bent to my chest.

The women aren't quiet. The walls are thin.
They open the cabinets to
comment on the ample food supply,
the foreign products—ones I brought.
"Have you seen anything like this
at the market? How can they afford it?"

Did they come when they
                                                    knew the house
would be empty? Are they part of the
인민반, a type of neighborhood watch,
the ones Byeong-ho warned me about?

The door to Byeong-ho's
          room opens,
                    and one of them enters. She
shuffles some things around on his shelves.
Then she takes
          a few steps in my direction.

                                          I don't breathe, feel like I
          might pass out from
holding my breath.

Her hand clutches the knob on the armoire;
it's loose, the hardware rattles.

The other woman yells,
"Come out!
They might be here soon."

I hear the front door close behind
them. It takes a minute before I can
stop the tears and calm myself
enough to climb out of my hiding place.
But I still hear them talking;
their laughter contrary to my fear,
their cackles skipping along
my every nerve.
They're sitting on the steps.
I creep closer.

"Oh, right. You weren't here
                    when they came.
The story is
Byeong-ho's father worked
in the Capital, for the government.
I don't know
his title, but it was important.
He was accused of giving
State secrets to the enemy."

The other woman gasps. "Was he..."

“Executed? No.
He was sent to a prison camp. But
he died not long after.”

“Why weren’t Oak-hee and Byeong-ho sent
with him?”

“I’m not sure.”

“Then it can’t be true. They wouldn’t
be here if it were.”

“It is true,” the woman insists.

“How was he caught?”

“This is the interesting part. There
was a foreign girl at Mangyongdae Funfair,
and she was there
with them.”

“A foreign girl?” I can hear
the doubt in her voice.
“You’re making things up.”

“I’m not! I’m not. My cousin told me all
about it when she visited from the Capital.
She saw Oak-hee and recognized her.

My cousin's husband worked
with her son. She was
so shocked to see her,
there was no denying
she was telling the truth.
There were several witnesses
at the park that day."

"What about the foreign girl?"

"She was captured and taken away. But
nobody knows what happened to her."

"How did she get there? Where
were her parents?"

"Nobody knows."

I always wondered if I'd had any effect
on the places I've traveled—
my own Butterfly Effect.
But this isn't a minute ripple caused by
the flutter of delicate wings.

If I hadn't gone to the park that day,
Byeong-ho's father
might still be alive.

They might still be living
comfortably
in Pyeongyang.
Byeong-ho might have gone to college,
might have been
assigned to an important position, too.

Halmeoni wouldn't have lost her son.

It feels like two hands are
squeezing the air from my lungs.
I hold back tears and the sounds that want to
escape from me.
Byeong-ho's feelings
toward me finally make sense.

He'd tried to help me
that day.
He'd told me to stay
behind the bushes,
to wait for his return.
But I didn't listen.
"Oh, hello. Sorry for the wait.
Did you need something?"
It's Halmeoni. Her tone more wary
than I have ever heard it.
I peek out the window to see
her standing at the threshold of
the gate they left open.

“We came to check on you.”

“We heard you were sick.”

“We brought some strawberries.
We know
you like them.”

“Thank you for your concern.
I am doing well today,” she says, but
her breathing is labored.
“And I got some strawberries of my own.”
She pats the bag on her shoulder. “You two
can go. I’m sure you have plenty to
do with your time.”

“What else did you buy?” one pries.

The other, “Where’s Byeong-ho?”
“He was sent for spring planting.”
She gives them
curt, polite replies, cutting
their inquiries short.

Once they leave,
she opens the door,
gestures for me to be quiet, and

searches the house, as I
point out everywhere they'd been.
She gives the all clear and
settles down on the mattress.

Everything that's been building inside
my chest releases as I fall to my knees,
my forehead touching the edge
of the quilt, sobs racking my body.
I attempt an apology that will never be enough.

Halmeoni hits my arm, telling me to get up.
But it's too weak. She's too weak.
"*Aish,* I'm going to rip their tongues out
for talking about us,
coming to our house. Sit up and look at me."
Her body is weak,
but her voice is strong.
I stare at her with a mascara-
stained face, my hair
stringy, pieces
of it stuck to my wet cheeks,
and I fight
to catch my breath.

She takes my hand,
her skin paper-thin,
the fingertips, once calloused,
now smooth like flower petals.

"It's not your fault. You
didn't know to listen to
Byeong-ho, to stay
hidden."

"But Halmeoni, how did you escape?"
연좌제. Guilt by association—the law
under which generations are
punished for the crimes
of family members.

"My son sent us out of the city
before they could show up
at our door. He bribed
the officials—his friends—
with all the money he had,
so we would only be
banished from the Capital,
so he would be sent
to the prison camp,
instead of executed.
He had saved a lot.
And money goes a long way."

"But at that time…" I dread
imagining what they might have had
to do to survive
during the famine. "Were you okay?"

She pats my hand.
"We made it through.
I know you're just hearing it,
but it was a long time ago,
and I don't like to think about those days."

I nod slowly, still filled with guilt
and shame. All because I shouted his name.

Halmeoni insists I let her watch a drama
until she falls asleep, exhausted from whatever
she's been doing this morning, but it's really
a distraction for us both.
Before I leave, I set the USBs and SD cards
on top of the chest in Byeong-ho's room.
The least I can do is give him
what he asked for.

———

Halmeoni,
then

Byeong-ho comes home from school, and
tells me more of his friends
have stopped showing up.
He may be one of them
soon. He is hungry.

His bones
show too much;
his father would be angry.

Perhaps starvation
has already
claimed my son.
Perhaps illness
or violence. It's just
Byeong-ho and me now. Soon our family
might be down to one. Down from three,
down from five.
My grandson shivers beneath
the blanket, his body beside me, sharing warmth
as our cells burn the last
of their reserves.

If I could

cross into China,

I'd find work,

make money, and bring

it back to take

care of him.

Eighteen

I spend the next two days in bed.
Sometimes Timothy is there with me.
It's easy to fall back into him.
I called; he came.
I told him everything.
He tries to hug away my shame, holding
me. Even though
I didn't know better, it doesn't change

what happened
to Byeong-ho
                    and Halmeoni.

All I can do now is cry,
          angry—
                    no amount of
                    anything I do can
                    make it up to
                    them.

Nothing can
bring back the
dead.

Bea is surprised to see Timothy
leave our apartment as
she returns from a work trip.

She slips into my room, a wide
grin spreading on her face.
A different response than when
he'd texted *Happy Birthday*.

"What's going on?" she asks
plopping onto my bed. "Why
was he here?"

I know she wants to hear
good things that make a heart
flutter and shiver,
but it's not like that.
I tell her everything,
and while she holds
me, she doesn't say it's okay,

doesn't minimize the
damage. She sits with
me.

She's known Byeong-ho
since she was fourteen,
my boy crush we had
to find when we
moved to Korea. He is some-
one I've always held
in my heart.
We have wondered
about his life,
his story.
Now, we
know.

Nineteen

It's been a few weeks
since I've spoken to
my mother, the both
of us avoiding anymore
laborious dead-ends.

I am grateful for what
she told me. I can appreciate
how hard it must have been
for her
with me.
I don't know
what I would have done
with a disappearing child.

But when I tried to share
about Halmeoni,
there was only
jealousy,

then nothing,
for three weeks.

Now, it’s a day to celebrate.
Gabby planned a Mother's Day
brunch, extending the invitation
to Bea and her mom as well.
Bea’s mom is great, but
she thinks I am
flaky—
all the times I’ve been late or haven’t
shown up. Bea tries
to cover for me, but she is
not a woman of
excuses.

Today I am on time. But they are
early, of course.
Gabby, Bea, and her
mom, already seated
at a table near two large
windows. The southern sun’s
light pours in,
soaking
the space freely, ready
to thaw any icy mood,
until

our mother
walks in; and she's
                    not alone.
Professor
Charles
Scott
holds the door open
and leads her by the hand.

I tap Bea's
foot and indicate,
she should look behind her.

I guess *take some time apart*
did not in fact mean *let's never*
                    see each other
          again.

"Did you know he
was coming?" I whisper
to Gabby. She shakes
her head *no*.

When they reach the table, my sister forces
a smile and says, "Professor Scott,
we didn't know you'd be
joining us."

"Oh, call him Charles,"
our mother says. "He
wanted to come and
meet everyone."

"He's already met us,"
I can't help but say and stare
directly.
But he doesn't waver. His smile
never falters, and there's a gleam
in his eyes.

"Not Bea and her mom," he
says, extending his hand to
her mother, a strong grip,
shaking in the shadow
of the floral centerpiece.

His face is
determined,
like he dares
me or Bea to
say something.
Like he's certain
we won't.

If Gabby knew,
she would
roundhouse kick him

into the street,
to land beside the other
trash.

But it is up to me and Bea.
I place a scone on her
plate. If she does the same,
we're in agreement. We
look at each other,
smirks pulling at the edges
of our mouths. I should
be thinking about my
          mother's feelings, especially
today. But Bea returns
the gesture, setting a crumbling
scone on my plate.

The mothers sit together,
Charles facing them.
I can't see him easily
with Gabby between us. But he
can stare at Bea
as much as he wants.

He smiles at her, then
grabs his knife, and
butters my mother's biscuit.

My fingertips pluck
the tines of a fork.

"Wait, I remember," Bea's mom
says. She asks her daughter,
"Didn't you have Professor Scott?"
"Mhmm," she confirms. "But
he wasn't very good."
Bea laughs
so they'll think it's a joke, but I choke
on my juice. Her mother blushes.

Charlie chuckles. "It's a shame you think
so. You were one of my best
students."

My mother's brow furrows.
"I thought you said
you'd never met
before."

"She's come back to me,
just now."
He smiles, the wrinkles
around his mouth trying to smooth out
his mistake.

"So, Charles,"
the name rolls over
Bea's tongue like a spiked marble.
"How's your wife these days?"

My mother's head snaps in
her direction. "He's divorced.
I wouldn't date a married man."
She laughs nervously, smiling
at Bea's mom.

"Neither would I," Bea says.
"But when I dated Charles, he was
still married. Of course, I didn't
know, because of all
the lies. Like the one he's telling now."

My mother sets her knife down,
the clink loud against
the plate. She stares at the man
across from her, a look
I've only seen her give my father.
"You dated one of your
students?"

Bea's mother pulls her shoulders back.
"You dated my daughter?
As her teacher and
a married man?"

His jaw drops open, then closes,
then opens again as he searches
for a denial,
a plausible excuse.

Every maternal muscle at the table
                    coiling, Bea's mother says,
                              "Get out
                                        of here
                    right now,
                              before I break every
          one of these
plates
                    over your head."

My mother, "How dare you
                              come in here, pretending
                    like you
                              don't know her."

Bea's mom glares while
gripping a knife in her fist,
cursing him in Korean.

He stands,
tossing the napkin from his lap. "I'll call
you later," he says to my mom.

She shakes
her head. "Don't bother. But I will
be calling
the university, on behalf of
all your students."

Pride fills my chest in a way
I've never felt
toward my mother.

Twenty

Bea went somewhere
to be alone.
It's what she needs,
so I give her space. I don't want
to impose any more
than I already
do.

Timothy is with his mom
and brother today, so I turn to
work.
It would be nice to take Halmeoni
out for brunch. I imagine
                    her in a pretty dress,
one that would go with
the sweater I crocheted
as a gift.

Then, instead of sitting on my bed,
I'm on their front steps. A heavy

moon hangs low in the sky.
It's so big, it lights
the whole courtyard. And the stars
are easy to see. No
pollution, fine dust, or city lights
to obscure the view.

It's been a few days since my last
visit. Did Halmeoni tell Byeong-ho
I know the truth?
I suddenly feel cold,
afraid
to face him.

There's a cough, and he appears
from the side of the house.
He startles when he looks up
and sees me.

He takes a deep breath,
hand on his chest. "Lina,
what are you doing here?"
He knows it's a dumb
question, but still asks.

Lina,
not *Angel.* I told them
my preferred name, but
he's never used it before.

The moonlight casts
a soft glow over his features.
He is handsome,
hair disheveled from sleep.
I can see the little boy in his face,
the one
I unknowingly destroyed.

"Come in," he says.

Before I can stop myself, I lower
to my knees in
apology.

"Get up," he says roughly.
"Get up."

I shake my head.
"You have every right to hate me.
What I did was
                    unforgivable.
I'm sorry," I say.
I'm sorry
I'm sorry
I'm sorry
and tears
begin
to flow
again.

He grabs me firmly by
the shoulders, tries to lift
me up.
He steps away, tells me to go
inside, and heads out
the gate.
When he realizes
I'm following him,
he spins around and
commands I
"Go back."

"You go back," I tell him. "It's your
house. I'll stay outside, and
leave you alone."

He glares at me, but
then sighs. "Let's go.
Get inside."
Before we move,
there are footsteps and
a man's voice puffs from behind
the glow of a cigarette.
"Byeong-ho,
is that you?"

Byeong-ho's eyes meet mine.
He pulls up my hood, then turns around
to greet the man who seems

like he's been drinking. I hide
my face behind Byeong-ho's
back, looking down
and away from the man.

"Who's with you? A
girlfriend?" I can hear the
smile in his voice. "That's good.
That's good. Won't you
introduce us?"

Byeong-ho's body stiffens,
his arm coming back to shield me.
He bows slightly to the man,
while I turn further away,
apologizing, explaining I am
very shy.

"You two fighting?"
He must have heard us.
"Don't fight. Byeong-ho, just
tell her she's right. Women
usually are, anyway. Good
advice from an old married
man." He chuckles.

Byeong-ho steps carefully backward,
bringing us closer to the gate.

He laughs and jokes with the
man, promising him we won't
fight anymore.

The man stumbles and falls.
"Let me help you," Byeong-ho
offers. He tells me to go, and
this time I listen.
I find Halmeoni
peacefully asleep.

Byeong-ho returns fifteen
minutes later. "Thank you,"
he says. "For what
you left me." He means
the USBs.

He closes
his bedroom door, putting
a paper-thin barrier between us.

I tuck the sweater under the
blanket beside Halmeoni.
Four-thirty in the morning,
I think I will not be here
when she wakes.

But I am. When her eyes open at six,
we play a card game in whispers,
trying not to disturb Byeong-ho.

If she were feeling well, they
might already be on their way
to the market to sell
some of the first fruits
from the garden,
the contraband
I provided, if
he hasn't sold them already.
As I think of him, he appears,
dressed for the day.
He carries Halmeoni on
his back to the outhouse.

They return as rain
begins to hit the roof.
Halmeoni settles onto her mat
while I prepare breakfast.

As I hand her a bowl of rice,
there is a
banging
on the gate.
It comes again, and a man
calls out, "Cha! Byeong-ho!"

Byeong-ho is on his feet,
telling me to hide, and
I disappear
into his room, crouching
in a corner because
the wardrobe is now full
of foreign products: small electronics.
I hug my knees, hoping they will not
search the house.
There is no air inside
my chest. I cannot breathe.
I should have gone inside
last night when
he told me to.

They pound
                    and shout his name again.

I hear the screech of the gate
as Byeong-ho unlocks it. The steps
of more than one person rush inside.

Halmeoni speaks to me through the door.
"Are you still there?"

          The front door is thrown open.
Three sets of footsteps—
two and Byeong-ho—

They demand to search the house;
they do not state
a reason.

Byeong-ho attempts to stall them.
"My grandmother is ill." She coughs
for effect. "She needs her rest. Please,
can we speak outside?" They're
not interested in what he has to say.

The door to his room slides open. He attempts
to keep them from entering,
but they
grab him around the neck and pull
him away.
Halmeoni from the other room, is
begging
them to stop.

A man takes a step in.
Our eyes meet, and
I disappear.

Home
in my bed.

———

Byeong-ho,
then

Angel's here! Angel's
here! She just appeared.
I run to find Halmeoni.
I'll have to tell her secretly,
without Appa hearing. He's
talking with Seong-chul's appa, and
Halmeoni is sitting on the bench
near them. I am
supposed to be hiding
from Seong-chul, but
Angel is in my hiding
spot. Her eyes are the
same green and gold
I used to think
was weird. She is weird.
Where has she been?
I sometimes forget she's
real, except when
Halmeoni mentions her.

But why is she here
where she can be seen?
She never appeared to us
outside
our home.

I run so fast to Halmeoni's
side, bending down, cupping
my hand around my mouth to whisper in her ear,
"Angel's here,"
as quietly as I can,
adrenaline running
through me.
Her eyes grow wide, and
she jolts, taking my hand.
"Where?" she asks, gesturing
for me to lead her.
We walk quickly, not running like
our hearts desire,
not wanting to draw
attention.

As we round
the corner, following
the paved path,
there are murmurs
from the people.
Hushed voices and
pointed fingers show
us what they're
talking about.
Angel has been
caught, captured,

by two officers
who are dragging—
carrying—her.
Only her feet touch
the ground
when she kicks
against them.
Halmeoni and I stop,
watching Angel in
distress—she and us—
before we can decide
what to do. My father's firm
grip is on both our arms.

Angel sees me.
Halmeoni attempts to take
a step toward her, but my father
pulls her back, and
she falls to the ground.

She rubs her wrist.
I look back at Angel, and she cries
my name
as the men take
her in the opposite
direction. I move to run
to her, but my father stops
me, his fingers tight
around my arm.

I struggle against him,
my head hitting his chin. He curses
and wraps me tight;
not the same
as when I was young. He is not
full of affection, but fear. And
I am no longer
little.
We trip and fall
to the ground next to Halmeoni.
And Angel is gone.

Halmeoni and I are in tears,
and everyone stares,
a heavy blanket of
suspicion.

"That's enough!" my father
says to us. "Stop crying.
                                        Get up.
                              Follow me.
            Quickly."

Twenty-One

Byeong-ho,
now

"*Heok!* What was that?"
I hear the man exclaim
from my room. "Where'd she go?"

The one who is restraining me
loosens his grip, pushes me to
the floor, goes to investigate.

Halmeoni's eyes meet mine, and
all
        the tension in
                my body
                       dissipates.

We play dumb when they question us,
and the men argue, the one not believing
the other. But they're shaken, though they act

tough. They search
the house, ordering
Halmeoni to get up, so they
can toss her blanket and mat.
A sweater falls out, and they question
who it belongs to, where it came from.

Drunk Kim Cheol must have
blabbed to his wife,
because these men ask me
where my girlfriend is,
where she's from, if
she has a permit to visit—knowing
she doesn't—
why she sounds like
                    a foreigner.

                                                  They want to take me in
                              for questioning.

                              Appa was taken
                    for questioning
and never came home again.

I refuse when they come to grab me.
"I need to stay with Halmeoni.
You see, she can barely stand!"
They glance at each other, then size me up.
"What will you give us?"

They already made me pack
up all the goods in my closet.
The only thing
I have left of value
I buried in the garden.

They could use it against me,
    but I think they will use
    me instead.

One of them follows
me outside; the other stays in
the doorway, out
of the rain, which has slowed to a drizzle.

I dig in the wet dirt and pull up
the plastic bag
of SD cards and USBs.

I want to keep one or two
for myself, but
as I try to open the bag,
the officer knocks me on the head
and snatches it from my hand.

He grins.
"If these aren't real,
we'll be back.

And if they are,
we'll be back
for more."

He laughs, and flicks his cigarette
into the hole
I just dug.

Twenty-Two

After work, my mother
        invites herself
        over. She wants
to debrief regarding the professor.
She sits the three of us down—
Gabby, Bea, and myself—
while she paces.
She has become the professor, lecturing.
"If you had told me
                immediately,
we could have avoided
such a public spectacle.
We could have spared
Ms. Ji-eun from the mortifying truth."

"Actually," Bea interjects,
"I'm glad my mom knows."

"Still." My mother's eyes narrow.
"We could have plotted
a much better revenge."

"Revenge?" Bea's jaw hangs.

My mother claps. "Angel,
are you even listening?
It's like you're in
another state."

I am

worried

about what the State
has done to them.

"You need to pay
attention," she says.

"It's not her…" my sister
hesitates,

"fault."

"I'm sure
she can admit
she's at least partially

responsible
for what
happened.

Angel, what are you
thinking about?

That old lady?"

My head snaps up,
and our eyes
meet.
"I knew it!" my mother bites.
"She's
all you care about.
My,
my, even more than your own
family."
I stare past her, our one family
portrait on a shelf, toddler me
smiling.
Saved by a gentle rapping
on the door; he enters before

I have to answer.

"Timothy…?
Timothy!"
My mother's tone transforms,
dripping with honey.

I can't accept

that I might never see them again.

Twenty-Three

Days later, when I do,
when it happens and I show up
in their yard and see their faces
                    shining in the sun,
                              Byeong-ho is still healing
          from whatever was done
to him.
I burst into tears.
                    They're still here.
                    They're still
                    here.

I run to Halmeoni, and she wraps me in her arms,
like the first day.
Byeong-ho makes his way
to us, slowly; she tugs him into the embrace,
patting both our backs in
a grand display of strength.

This time,
it's not for a few
hours, but days.
Three,
the longest I have stayed
anywhere.

I should think
about my family,
Bea, Gabby, Timothy,
how frantic they must be.
But
I don't want to leave Halmeoni's side.

Byeong-ho and I work well
together. We don't say much,
except for what is essential
to care for Halmeoni
and each other.
I make sure he
eats and takes breaks;
he does the same for me.
When he speaks, not his
words, but his tone
says, "I'm glad
I'm not alone.
I'm glad you're here."

All my devices have died,
the portable chargers too, so
Halmeoni isn't able to
watch the final episodes
of our current drama.
I tell her
how it ends,
and her eyes close
as she listens.
She smiles,
pleased
with the
happy
ending.

She says
Byeong-ho and me
being together beside her is
          her happy ending.

Byeong-ho's eyes meet
mine, as I blink back
tears. He swallows
a lump in his throat.
We each hold one of
her tiny hands.

Since then,
she has rapidly
declined.
She stopped eating two
days ago. She won't
drink much. I should
have gone to medical
school, like my father.
But I'd imagined disappearing
in the middle of treating
a patient, in the middle
of a surgery, and now
I can't care for Halmeoni
like I want to. An IV, pain
medication, comfort measures;
all I can give
is my fleeting presence.

Byeong-ho brought a local
physician to see her yesterday,
while I hid in his room.
The man said there was
nothing to do except be
with her until
the end.
We paid for him
to tell us what we already knew.

Halmeoni is hurting. She
doesn't say it—she doesn't
say anything—but her face
and her body
tell us. Byeong-ho and I
squeeze her legs and arms, trying to
relax her nerves. She
sleeps for a little while,
until
she's jolted awake from
more sharp pain.

It's evening, the third day.
I just watched the sun set
from the front steps,
the sky shifting
into its steadfast blend
of pastel watercolors.

I return to my place
beside Halmeoni,
telling Byeong-ho he can take
a few minutes
for himself,
but before he can stand,
Halmeoni speaks,
her voice fragile.
"Byeong-ho."

He lowers his head,
so his ear is closer
to her lips. She takes
a wheezing breath.
"I'm so sorry I
left you back then. And that
I'm leaving
you now."

Halmeoni,
then

The river was frozen
when I crossed, the ice
black, slippery and stinging cold.

An old 조선족 man, an ethnic
Korean living in China,
whose wife has passed away
hired me to keep his house,
cook, and tend the garden,
while he works in the rice paddies.
I sleep in his daughter's old room;

she moved to
the city.
So easily

I've gained weight, but

every bite of food tastes

bitter. Byeong-ho is

there, across the river.

surviving,

I hope.

I told him to

do what he can.

Hang around the marketplace,

don't be ashamed to beg,

and if that doesn't work,

don't be afraid to take.

Just for now,

until I can get back

to him,

weighed down by guilt and

the money in my pocket.

Twenty-Four

Byeong-ho hugs her,
his sobs falling with his tears against
her chest, assuring
her he's
okay.
    It was okay.
        He'll be okay.

I sit
as witness.

After a minute, he raises
himself away, knowing
it's already difficult for
her to breathe without his
added weight.
He gets up and walks
outside, trying to hide
his face as he goes.
Halmeoni grips my

arm; it's my turn
to get close and listen.
She says, "I was always
happy to see you here.
Then, that day,
and now.
Keep coming
to Byeong-ho,
if you can."

"I will," I say in her ear.

I stroke her hair
and kiss her forehead.
She doesn't open her eyes,
but the borders of
her mouth peak
into a soft smile.

Byeong-ho returns,
sits cross-legged across
from us. We stay
in silence, waiting,
watching her breaths.
Two hours pass
            before it stops.
He checks her pulse,
puts his ear to her chest,
then sits back up.

She's gone.
Halmeoni's fingers are still warm
in my hand, in his hand too. We
each hold onto her, clinging to
the memory of life.

I open my mouth,
to utter some measure of comfort,
but all I can do is choke on sobs,
my tears running alongside
Byeong-ho's.
A question comes from
an audible voice, "Lina,
why are you crying?"

Timothy. I'm home, on my knees,
in the middle
of my living room. He sits
down in front of me, one leg
on each side, surrounding me with
his body, his arms around my shoulders,
pulling me into his chest.

"What's wrong?
Where have you been?
I've been waiting
                            here
                                        for you.
         We've all been waiting."

"Oh, thank God," I hear my
father say. When I pull away
from Timothy, my father is
on the couch, rubbing
sleep and possibly tears
from his eyes.

"Your mom and Gabby are
in your bed," Timothy explains.
"When you didn't come home,
we had to tell your parents
the truth about where you've been."

My mother is so relieved
I've returned,
but is also furious
at me,
my
condition,
my lack
of control,
my
secrets.
To go
from three days
of silent vigil
to my mother's roaring—
I have no
capacity for it.

"We didn't know if
you were alive or dead!
You could have at least
called us!"

"She can't
call from North Korea,
Connie," my father says, and the
bickering begins.

I take myself
into the
bathroom,
lock the door,
and run
the water.
I barely hear Bea
when she says
she'll bring me
clean clothes.

I stand in the shower,
knowing
Byeong-ho
is alone.

Gabby changes the
sheets on my bed,
and I crawl into

them. Mom and Dad
have left. They'll check back in
later,
separately.

I tell the other three
to go to work,
but Bea
doesn't have outside
work, so she stays in
the bed beside me,
working on her laptop.
I drink some tea
and fall asleep, thinking
of Byeong-ho left alone
with Halmeoni's body.

Twenty-Five

It's been a few days.
Everyone keeps
checking on me.
Is anyone checking
on Byeong-ho?

They sit
with me and tell me
I don't have
to talk about it. But
I want them to ask.
I want them to help
me cement the
memories I have
of her in
my mind.
I want to talk
about her,
about him,
and that place.

I've willed myself to
go back several times,
but it doesn't work.
My mother's theory
is wrong.
She hasn't talked to me,
but she keeps texting Bea,
Gabby, and Timothy
for updates. She cares,
in her own way.
I accept
the degree to which
she can handle
me.

Tonight, I help
Timothy clean the kitchen, and
I disappear.
But I'm not in
their house or their yard.
I'm at the foot of a mountain.

Morning's not fully awake, just yawning
and fog hangs
heavy, an all-encompassing shroud,
so that I cannot see.

"You came,"
Byeong-ho says.

His voice startles me,
then he appears,
his face
a few inches from mine.
He looks like
he hasn't slept.
"I just finished
burying her."

"By yourself?"

"Yes. No one else is here.
If it were winter, the ground
would have been frozen.
She waited for spring
to make it easier
                    for me."
He leads me a few feet toward
the foot of Halmeoni's grave.

We kneel and bow
our foreheads to the
the ground. We stay
a long time, until
he begins to cry, and I
embrace him. His hands are dirty,
so I wipe
his tears with
my own.

We can't walk back
to the house; I might
be seen. So, we
hike up
the mountain, the fog
thinning as we climb.
At the top, we sit
and look to the rising sun.

He brought strawberries with him,
and he hands me
one. "What happened
to my father, I blamed you for a long time,
          and I know you've been blaming yourself.

"But it would have happened either way.
I heard him talking with a friend—
They were looking for a reason
                              to remove him
          from his position.
          If you hadn't come,
                         they would have created one.

"Halmeoni and I should have been taken too.
He leveraged everything he could—
every possession, every man he knew
with any sense of loyalty to him—
for us to be spared and sent
to the countryside.

There were times I wished we would have
died, never experienced life outside
the city.

"But it's not your fault. I didn't
mean what I said about your gift.
I'm grateful it brought you
here. You don't need to apologize.
You don't need to feel bad about it.
                                    And neither do I."

I let his words sink in. It
will be a long time before
they reach my ocean floor.

"I wish you didn't have to go," he says.
"It's better—safer—if you do, but..."
He trails off,
staring at the horizon.

I think of Halmeoni's last
request. *Keep coming
to Byeong-ho,
if you can.* I know
          and must accept
it's not up
                    to me.

After some quiet moments
listening to birds, watching
the fog vanish, banished
by the glory of the sun,
I appreciate the beauty
I could not explore before.
I hand Byeong-ho the bag
from my shoulder.
"If you ever decide to leave
this place, you'll find
things in here that
might help you."

He takes it, doesn't look
inside, sets it aside,
and stays with me there
until I disappear.

Twenty-Six

These days
I live
in a sadness no one
around me understands.

They are unfamiliar
with the person
          I will always miss
who has passed
from life
          to death.

I have not returned
since the funeral.
I've been to
Cairo, Bolivia,
Sweden, the
Caribbean.
But I have not been taken
back there.

Timothy wants
my heart to be
with him, though he doesn't
say it.
He's being patient,
but the old
distance and doubt
is setting up house
in his mind
again.

This time, he is
not wrong.

I flew to Incheon, rode the subway to Paju,
to the border, to use
binoculars—as if I could
see and
will myself to be
there too. But
nothing happened.

Every day,
I get up and dress with
the hope that
maybe today
will be the day,
          I visit Byeong-ho.

Twenty-Seven

I'd had crushes before,
gone on dates before,
always keeping them at a distance
because of my condition.
But Timothy wasn't like them;
he knew
                    and pursued
what he wanted: me.
More time with me,
more whispers behind the
bookshelves in the library,
more sprints through the
rain back to his car, more
warm kisses under the
lamp post outside my dorm,
more summer nights with
fireworks and fried chicken.
                    More. Always
                              more than I could give.

All I had were excuses:
why I was late,
why I didn't return his call, why
I missed class, why I missed
so much. He didn't know the
truth
          yet. I was terrified
          to tell him, for him
          to find out.

It was Christmas Eve. I was supposed to meet
his mother for the first time. As I walked
to the restaurant, warm tingles
spread across my skin
and I ended
up outside a Catholic church
in France. Snow crunched
beneath my boots as I climbed
the brick steps to attend
a midnight mass that had
already begun. While I sat
in the pew, counting the minutes
until my return, Timothy
          called Bea because he
                    had seen me
                              vanish.
He could have run then,
but he didn't. He'd pressed in.
He'd kept me. And I'd kept him.

Tonight, another Christmas Eve, we
had dinner with my family, opened
presents at my mom's, now
heading back to my place. But
something feels
out of place, has been
off
          for a while.

"Are you okay?" he asks,
putting the car into park.

Staring out the window, I ask,
"What does it mean to be okay?"

"I don't know." A vexed look
crosses his face, and he gestures
at me. "Not this."

"What is *this*?" I ask.
I want him
to say what he sees.

"Lina, you're never *present*
when we're together. We already
have so much time taken
from us because of your traveling.
But where is your mind these days?"
He knows where it is. He just

doesn't want
confirmation my thoughts
are consumed with concern
for another man. But
                    that's not all.

I turn and face him, close
the air vent blowing in my eyes.
"When you asked me to marry you
before, that was all I wanted.
But now, I don't think
I've forgiven you for leaving me.
I don't trust you
                              won't do it again.

"You need more than
I can give. I can't love you like you
want or need, and I don't want to feel I'm
constantly disappointing someone
for the rest of my life.
I won't
feel guilty because
of my gift anymore.
I won't be
burdened, be
with someone who's
burdened
by it."

He reaches for my hand,
makes a few feeble attempts
to persuade me. But his heart
isn't in it, and neither is mine.
I give him
a hug, tell him he can
come by to get his stuff another day,
wish him 'Merry Christmas,' and
watch him drive away.

I can see
my breath and wonder
if Byeong-ho is alive and warm enough
                    wherever he is.

Twenty-Eight

Byeong-ho,
now

As I round each corner, scale another flight of
stairs, overhead lights click on, motion-detected,
the electricity my favorite part; I've never known
a city that does not sleep. I always keep
a light on. I know how
much Halmeoni hated darkness.
I have bad dreams about burying her
where no light reaches. But she has
the sweater from Lina
to keep her warm.

I head downstairs
to the convenience store
across the street, ready to eat
and finally reach
out to her.
It has been almost a year.

It took some time
to get here.
The cherry blossoms
will bloom soon. Her birthday
is coming up.

She never came back.
I waited, and the officers
came to threaten me
again, demanding more
than I was willing to give,
what Lina had given me—
USB sticks, money, maps, contacts.
I put them off, promising
I would get them something, giving
myself time to leave.

Today, in this
new place,
I got a job
promotion. It's something
good
I can share.
I stare at her picture
on KakaoTalk.

Knowing her doesn't have
    to be a secret anymore.
We could walk in the street, eat

at a restaurant, be seen
together.

But she has
probably moved
on, is happy. And that is all
I want.

I will call to thank her,
and that will be all.

I press
the button.
My heart beats
along with the ringtone.

"Hello?"
Her voice is hesitant,
doubtful.

"It's me."

She gasps, then exhales
relief.
"Where are you?"

"Seoul."

"Are you okay?

Do you want me to—?"

"Yes. Will you come?"

"I'm coming.

I'll be there

soon."

Rachel Langley is a Georgia native with a degree in communications and professional writing. She's always had a love for words, languages, and storytelling, finding great satisfaction in bringing characters to life on the page.

She is the author of the *Struck Trilogy*, a new adult sci-fi/fantasy series; *Struck* was a finalist in the IAN Book of the Year Awards. *In the Coming and Going* is her debut adult fiction novel.

rachellangley.com

facebook.com/rach3llang/

Instagram: @langleywrites

Printed in the USA
CPSIA information can be obtained
at www.ICGtesting.com
JSHW021537171124
73775JS00005B/13

9 798991 579612